Borrowed Light

Borrowed

Light

a novel by LISA SCHAMESS

SOUTHERN METHODIST UNIVERSITY PRESS Dallas

This novel is a work of fiction. Names, characters, places, and incidents are either the product of the author's imagination or are used fictitiously.

Copyright © 2002 by Lisa Schamess
First edition, 2002
All rights reserved

Requests for permission to reproduce material from this work should be sent to:
    Rights and Permissions
    Southern Methodist University Press
    PO Box 750415
    Dallas, Texas 75275-0415

Grateful acknowledgment is made for permission to quote from the following works:

"Here" by Robert Creeley is reprinted from *The Collected Poems of Robert Creeley, 1945–1975*, by permission of the University of California Press. Copyright 1983 by The Regents of the University of California.

"Deep in the Heart of Texas" by June Hershey and Don Swander. Copyright 1941 by Melody Lane Publications, Inc. Copyright renewed. International copyright secured. Used by permission.

Jacket photograph: Q Street Alley, near Dupont Circle, Washington, D.C., by Colin Winterbottom

Jacket design: Tom Dawson and Rich Hendel
Text design: Rich Hendel

Library of Congress
Cataloging-in-Publication Data
Schamess, Lisa, 1963–
Borrowed light : a novel / by Lisa Schamess.
   p. cm.
ISBN 0-87074-474-7 (alk. paper)
1. AIDS (Disease)—Patients—Fiction.
2. Washington (D.C.)—Fiction.
3. Terminally ill—Fiction. 4. Architects—Fiction. 5. Gay men—Fiction. I. Title.
PS3619.C3255 B67   2002
813'.6—dc21   2002027639

Printed in the United States of America on acid-free paper

10 9 8 7 6 5 4 3 2 1

Dedicated to the memory of my parents

Acknowledgments

This book would not exist without the Jenny McKean Moore Fund for Writers. I began the book in a Fund-sponsored workshop in 1992 and completed the manuscript in 1995 during a Fund-sponsored fellowship at the Virginia Center for the Creative Arts (VCCA). My thanks to VCCA for that summer respite and for a second residency in 1996.

The Jenny McKean Moore Fund also introduced me to writers whose fine work sets an unapproachable example for me, and whose encouragement sustains me, including Faye Moskowitz (who founded the Fund), Carole Maso, Richard McCann, and Joyce Reiser Kornblatt. I am grateful for the voices of Michael Klein, Rebecca Brown, and Mark Doty, as well as of Paul Monette (of blessed memory), whose work inspired me during this project.

I am deeply indebted to my first and most important writing teachers: C. W. Smith of Southern Methodist University, and my father, Joseph Wormser. My husband, Gil Schamess, offered me the vital gifts of belief, love, and the unrelenting example of his moral and aesthetic rigor. I remain awkwardly grateful for his most precious trust: our daughter, Mona.

I thank my families—Wormsers, Brenners, Rosens, Krasnows, Schamesses, Schwartzes, Backs, Markewiches, and Sheingolds—for the stories they have given me with open hands. Andrew Schamess was especially instrumental and patient with my various medical queries. I thank my friends for their patience and careful reading, especially the Worth Our Salt Writers Group: Rebecca Flowers, Paulette Roberts, Carollyne Hutter, Eliza King, Anne Lindenfeld, and Paula Van Lare.

Southern Methodist University Press provided a wonderful homecoming for me. Kathryn Lang and George Ann Goodwin were wonderful to work with, as was my superb copyeditor, Robin Whitaker.

I would also like to thank Congregation Adas Israel and the D.C. Jewish Community Center—the 16th Street "J"—for the spiritual and physical space to write and for programs that supported me and my family in dark times and brought me deep friendships in brighter times. Sonia Cruz was there for my daughter and me day after day, without fail. A special thanks to Miriam Isserow and Yehuda and Ronee Goldman for so many Fridays and to Sue and Kali Hoechstetter for rainy days and Mondays. To my passionate friend Steve Linick, thank you for your careful reading and insights.

Last but never least, I am indebted to the impossible, irresistible Charles Edison Imhoof and his loving family. They know why.

What
has happened
makes

the world.
Live
on the edge,

looking.

—Robert Creeley, *Here*

1992

A man is dying in this quiet room. He simply keeps forgetting to breathe. Outside the day is sunny after a week of rain, in February, a Sunday, about ten o'clock. His ex-lover is with him, watching the violet numbers tumble slowly on the blood pressure monitor as they have done all night. At this particular moment, the former lover, whose name is Rich, is holding the hand of the dying man, whose name is David, and watching the half-open eyes glimmer with awareness, or just reflected light.

"It's all right," Rich repeats. "You can go." He waits for what he's been told to expect, the sound of last breath. He waits for David's body to seem suddenly less substantial or for there to be, definitively, one fewer presence in the room.

"Go ahead," he says, and waits, and looks up at the monitor, watching the flat line and the blinking box that says "APNEA." He waits for that last exhalation until he notices the nurse at the door.

"He's not breathing," he reports calmly.

"That's right, dear," says the nurse. "He's passed away."

You could ask to see the charts if you're a member of the family. Or you could write to the hospital to get his official record from a specialty firm in San Diego, at a small cost. The record contains his time and cause of death and a final write-up from his attending physician. Daily notes from doctors and nurses regarding the man's oncological, viral, neurological, and pain treatment are part of the record. You would have access to the reports from various work-ups conducted in the emergency room. You could read: "33 y/o WM brought into EU by

3

1992

friend, compl chest pains, diarrhea, low BP. PT is in adv stg AIDS with hist of CMV and four prior hosp. Mental status altered."

The emergency room notes contain the man's personal history, his profession, family, complaints. The report includes results of verbal tests of his fund of knowledge, which was found intact. He could name the nation's presidents all the way back to Eisenhower, and he remembered four out of four words at zero, one, and five minutes, but mental probes were difficult owing to the man's tangentiality and flight of ideas. You could read: "His proverbs were very concrete. His similarities were mildly impaired. He was often unable to get associations. His constructions were fair. He was oriented to person but not to place or time."

You would learn that the man was the older of two children, that his family had a history of heart disease and glaucoma, that his mother died of complications from heart disease six years prior to his hospitalization. You would learn that the man was not currently in a serious relationship, that he had bachelor's and master's degrees in architecture from the University of Virginia, and that he worked until ten months ago at a firm specializing in residential and small-scale commercial architecture.

The patient's record from his six days on the fourth floor of George Washington University Hospital includes amazingly intimate, sometimes intrusive facts: frequency of bowel movements, date of incipient renal failure, date of actual renal failure. You'd know that the patient had no prior directive on file, waiving claim to extraordinary life-saving measures in the event of terminal status. There is a single sentence marking what had been a lengthy argument between the patient's aged father and a night nurse: "Family refused further bloodwork." You would see how the orders for pain medication changed over the last six days of the man's life, from episodic relief to continuous comfort, all signed by Dr. Olu, the tall, nearly silent Nigerian anesthesiologist who taught the patient to say thank you in Aruba: *Oshai*.

The record leaves things out. It doesn't distinguish night from day. It doesn't presume to separate indignities from mere irritations. It misses the blunt wonder of the man's entering the emergency room near respiratory arrest, then recovering enough to sit up and greet

1992

friends, and finally lapsing into delirium and dying, all in a week's time. The nurses are all one nurse in the record: no Deborah with cool hands, no LaTonya who was studying computer programming, no Carl who always checked to make sure the patient's IV was still right and that his monitor pack wasn't tugging on his chest, even on the last day. There is no record of the dozen small seasons of gratitude, laughter, boredom, and despair that passed in that room. No chart of the slim, fractured sleep of the vigil.

Rich's nights at the hospital, restless on a cot at the foot of David's bed, were awful mimics of nights they used to spend together, anxious nights for Rich when he kept watch over a sleeping David. It should have been the opposite, he thought then; it should have been David awake, worrying for himself. But until last year, until David left him, Rich had carried the weight of fear, and even now he slept only a few grateful hours at a time until a nurse dragged a wedge of bright light in from the hall and bustled about David's motionless body. Then Rich pulled on his shoes and made his squinting way down the zealously waxed hallway to the cafeteria, to break up the night with coffee, or juice, or a bagel sealed in plastic from the vending machine. Sometimes he was so tired he just stood in front of the automatic carousel, clutching his dollar and watching food from his childhood go slowly around: bananas, cereal in boxes that could be cut open to serve as bowls, pint cartons of milk, and cheap cheese crackers. He brought his snacks back to David's room and sat on the edge of the cot, listening to the heat hiss through the closed vents under the window, the sighing of oxygen and suction, the odd chime of the heart monitor every half hour.

Early in the week they talked a little, if David was alert. Even a day or two before he died, they had simple exchanges. David had always, when he was falling in or out of sleep, made a soft huffing sound. When he did so now, in his narcotic twilight, Rich tried to catch it, to ride it toward words.

"What, darling? Is there something you want?"

"You should see this place."

"What place?"

David tried to turn his stiffened neck, tsked in irritation when he couldn't. "This *place*."

1992

Rich humored him. "The place you told me about?"

"Took you to. Didn't I? It's enormous. It's marvelous. I'm ready to move in."

"Tell me again what it's like."

Silence. Rich always lost him after a few moments, without warning.

There is no record of Henry's long daily walk to his best friend's last room, down the bright white corridor with its islands of blue tile in the floor. There is no report of Henry's dreams for years afterward, when he'd go down the bright hall again, shoes tapping the spotless surface, shadow swaying over square blue tiles. No note stood in the official file to indicate that David would be waiting in a dreamed doorway, packed to go home, impatient. Or sitting by an open window at the end of the hall—not the hospital's blinded hallway eye, but the open casement window on the staircase up to their old, steam-warmed apartment on Columbia Road. Sometimes Henry didn't find his friend in the hospital at all, but in a flea market or a grocery store, at his elbow suddenly, steering Henry toward some wise choice.

In the official record, "family" means David's father, who came late in the week, just in time. His walk down the hall was full of the faces of kindred spirits, families glancing out at him from other rooms or wearily meeting his eyes at their doorways. A yellow decal with a large blue eye marked his son's room. A nurse told him it was to indicate a patient liable to fall or wander. But the decal must have been up for days, or for another patient now gone, because by the time Walt got there, David's body barely rippled the bright wool blanket someone had put over it.

Two of David's friends were in the room when his father arrived. They introduced themselves and gave him their place by the bed.

"We have to go anyway," one of them said, "unless you'd like us to stay awhile? He wakes up sometimes." Walt didn't know if this was warning or encouragement.

"No, you go on. We'll be fine," he said.

The single straight-backed chair in the room was jammed between the bed and the window. David's face was turned that way. His eyes were heavy but half open. Had he blinked?

Walt came up to Washington on one of those rainy weekdays that

1992

make a man feel he can hear farther. The sound of the rain was in the room with them now, bringing in the sound of the cars whisking by, splashing pedestrians in intersections, the sidewalk vendors calling "*Um*-brella, *Um*-brella," stepping hard on the first syllable to make it stay put. Out in the hall, a doctor talked on the house phone, and someone jangled their keys in their pocket, ready to go home.

"Jodie will get here as soon as she can," Walt began. "Hang in there, son." From his overnight bag, Walt pulled out an envelope with the words *Uncle Buster* crayoned in brown, surrounded by decals of ponies and stars. "Gina made you some pictures. This one she calls The Happy Family. It's a bunch of faces, see? She says the one in the middle is you. Here's Gina riding a horse that's also a tree. And here's a clock. She'll be ready to tell time soon."

He propped the drawings up against the windows, behind the flowers someone had put in a bunch of urinal bottles. There were other tasteless touches around the room: Mardi Gras beads draped at the head of the bed, the rubber mask of Ronald Reagan on the IV pole. This wasn't a joke, to Walt. This wasn't funny. Under the wool blanket, under the hospital's starched sheets stamped with George Washington's face in blue ink, was his only son.

A wavy blue line jumped and flattened at the bottom of the screen showing David's heart rate and blood pressure. A nurse walked in without knocking.

"I'm his dad," Walt said. It was the only greeting that made sense to him.

"You look alike," said the nurse. She stood at the foot of the bed and put her hand on one of David's feet. "Can you hear me, sweetie? Sweetie-pie? Your dad's here. Want to let us know if you're awake?"

"Is he breathing on his own?"

"Oh yes. We're not putting any more machines on him. We have him on oxygen, just to make it more comfortable to breathe. Wake up, honey. You've got a visitor." The numbers on the monitor climbed a little, though David didn't move.

"He knows you're here," the nurse said. "Just say his name now and then."

1992

※

You could simply approach the family now, gathered in the waiting area with the dead man's hastily packed belongings. You could ask them a few questions. Families at such times are often happy to talk. Tell them you've lost a few souls yourself. Tell them they seem like nice people. And they do, talking and laughing (yes laughing, because one of them is imitating tall Dr. Olu, who has been kind enough to stop by daily, long after new pain orders were no longer needed, and who stopped by just now, to say how very sorry he was. It's this Dr. Olu, the quiet, kind pain doctor from Africa, whose musical dialect Henry is so cruelly and perfectly imitating: "You're going to feeeeeeel bether, my friend, you're going to feeeeeel motch, motch bether," so that even David's father can't stop laughing, until tears are slicking down from the corners of his eyes and wetting his sideburns).

What would you do — interrupt this scene of unfettered relief to ask for details that worry you alone, you who want to know so much about this man's death for the sake of previewing yours? Isn't it enough that they are laughing now, even though they have their own deaths approaching them like buses twinkling at the tops of hills, poised and still for moments that seem like always? What would you ask anyway? Who was there and what they saw? What he said? Whether they feel better? You can see they do. Or is the laughter a kinetic reaction, mere tension expressed that might as well be tears?

No, the laughter feels like something all its own, exuberant, full of light, breathing its own life until its own inevitable death, when this intimate knot in the waiting room will unravel and the individuals go their own way.

Follow any one of them. Past the nurses' station, down the elevator, through the lobby, out into the empty Sunday street. Follow David's father back to his hotel room and watch him undress in the dim afternoon light, the curtains drawn and no lights overhead, because that's how he lives at home, saving energy. He lies down on top of the bedcovers in his thin undershorts and T-shirt, gray with laundering, cocking both arms up beside his head and folding his hands underneath his bald skull, feet still in their black socks crossed at the ankles. Watch

1992

him all you want. He won't say anything. His eyes are open. You can tell he's thinking, or letting go of thoughts as they well up.

Maybe he's thinking back to a Sunday afternoon in Dallas, when David and Jodie were little more than babies. He lay in this position on the floor in front of his new high-fidelity stereo, listening to impossible, frenetic stretches of Paganini, when David came and tucked his head against one of Walt's biceps and rested his small hot hand on Walt's chest. Walt was only a little older than David was today. But he was already eight years married, ten years out of the service, feeling old that afternoon. How young he was, really, a young father, a young man. In the dim hotel room now—now—Walt knows what it is to be old. He might be trying to recall his son's voice at that age and for all the years after. Impossible to remember them all, because voices don't succeed each other clearly, not even in memory.

※

If you were to follow Henry and Rich, you would see them get into Henry's car and drive up K Street, through Glover Park and into Palisades. They park in front of Rich's ample Arts and Crafts home. He bought it last year, when he finally sold the house on 16th Street. Thanks to David's work, he made a nice profit. The new house has a wide, white wrap-around porch.

"What are those?" Henry points to the potted blue plants on each step.

"Lobelia. Spiderwort. And delphinium."

Henry comes inside because Rich asks him to, and sits at the kitchen table while the water boils for tea. Rich goes upstairs to wash and change out of clothes he's been wearing for two days. He pauses at his open bureau drawer, thanking God that all he can see are his own clothes, that David took all his things when he left. He examines his face in the mirror, not seeing himself exactly but formulating an idea of himself, a way he'd like to be for the rest of the day, for the rest of his life if only he could sustain it. From the top of the stairs he calls down to his friend, to David's friend who became his friend, to ask him to stay a while and let Rich take him to lunch.

Henry, who has the feeling that nothing needs doing right now as

1992

much as he needs to sit here and do nothing, says yes. Rich will turn on the shower, secure that he has company, and will step out of his dirty clothes and ball them into his hamper and slip under the spray with a sigh of purest pleasure, so happy in his bones to have survived, to be so dirty he'll know when he is clean. The soap seems to peel back an old skin he's been wearing, and the razor scrapes away his tired expressions: studious frowns for talking with doctors, tight smiles meant to reassure David, the aggressive chin-forward he wore when he phoned the insurance company or Medicare. He feels giddy showering and shaving in midday, as though preparing for an afternoon date.

Downstairs Henry marvels at this curious, almost new feeling that he has no place better to be. His feet don't shift under the table as they habitually do, his back feels all collapsed, and he is sore, but it is a good soreness, a racer's exhaustion. In Rich's pantry he finds a can of tuna and a box of crackers. He opens both and doesn't trouble to find mayonnaise. He stands at Rich's sink eating from the can, comforted by the clarity of his hunger and the fact of its satisfaction.

Rich, leaning in the kitchen doorway, has put on a clean black shirt and jeans. He pushes his wet hair back from his face. Henry can smell the soap and warmth across the room. They already know what's going to happen, because they have come to this place before out of the same pure need. There is no hurry. This has everything to do with David, as it did the other times. Maybe this time they will travel further than expected. Maybe they will wind up together somewhere, beginning from now. Henry sits down and drinks his tea.

"Want some chocolate?" Rich asks.

"You have some?"

"Truffles. I would have thought you'd sniff them out."

"Very funny."

Rich pulls down a box from a high shelf in the pantry. "I've been saving these," he says. "Emergency chocolates." He pulls his chair closer and brings his face near Henry's. "Help yourself."

※

Maybe you'd just rather stay at the hospital for a while, get more used to the idea of this death, and later go through the open door into

1992

the rest of your day. That's understandable. You just got here and the others had so much more time. Maybe you'd like to know how they could leave him, to know what finally edged them out of the room where the corpse still lies, in a room so silent—no more oxygen needed and no more monitors or drips. If you stay with the body, you might have the illusion it is still breathing, because how could it not, with a man's face and a man's hands and feet? You might feel very alone or not at all alone (opinions differ). You would certainly be asked to step outside when the technicians come to disconnect and move the remains. If you wait in the hall, you'll hear the vinyl tug and crunch of the hazardous-wastes bag being opened and manipulated, the zipping closed, and the shifting of the body from bed to gurney, the fluff and snap of a clean sheet, the pulling away of the man's last linens to be purified in the steaming waters of the basement laundry. You can stay in the hall as long as you like, overhearing the lives of the hospital workers and the families whose own vigils aren't ended. Watch the door to the dead patient's room: it will slip open and the body will be wheeled matter-of-factly past you, down the side hall to the service elevator. When the gurney passes, if you hold your breath and stay still, you might just feel the nearness of death's density, like the silent, white eye of a storm.

※

Try to remember how, out of habit perhaps, his eyes still turned toward light, so he died with his face to the window. Let's hope he wasn't completely blind, because, of all the patients who had lain there, he was the one who would have liked the view. Through the nail-marred, cracked, repainted edges of the window frame could be seen the simple face of the building wing across the way, broken regularly by identical paired windows with low double sashes. It was near the end of winter; he was too high up for any but the topmost branches of the courtyard trees to reach, and the trees were still bare. The planes of the building across the way met at a clean, shadowed edge such as the one he rested on himself, the meeting of sleep and waking, beaded with morphine.

As for the plain granite face of the opposite building, as for the

1992

naked trees, they would have suited him, he who had devoted his life to the rigor of sound structures. The gray view of building and branches might have seemed to him a blessing, an augury, a benediction on his unadorned life. A sturdy life that stood for what it was, for as long as it was.

1989

I grew up in the heart of flash-flood country—Dallas, Texas—where they taught us to duck and cover for tornadoes as well as the Reds. If a hard rain gave way suddenly to calm green sky, if an awesome stillness came into the air, you knew you were in for a twister. If it happened during the day, we schoolchildren would go berserk with joy and have to be restrained in our seats at recess, lest we go chase funnel clouds outside. This is one of the few ways I am still brave: I would gladly go running to see a cloud touch ground.

But before a stillness like the kind I am describing, there is rain like this, sluicing against the ground at a steady, workmanlike pace. I listen to it tacking away at the windowsill as I lie in bed and my beloved moves from room to room downstairs, closing windows, starting coffee. I stretch into the hollow his body just left, splaying my arms and legs wide into a perfect star, da Vinci's Proportional Man.

We were up late last night, playing Scrabble in the front room with the Weather Channel on, watching the forecasters chart the eastward path of the hundred-year floods in the Midwest. Now Rich's bare feet are on the stairs, coming close. He opens the door with one elbow, carrying two cups to the bed.

"Morning, love." He hands me mine.

"Morning. Thanks." I finger a trail of shaving lather from his chin. "Finally get some sleep?" There's a slender thread of blood in the shaving cream on my finger.

He kisses me. "Mm. So-so."

"You cut your chin."

He feels his face. "So I did." He chooses a suit for the day and snaps a fresh tie like magic from the dark closet. I drift, and then the room is light gray. Rich is gone. I dress myself for work, cinching my belt,

1989

unwrapping a new shirt with a narrower collar, putting on thick socks so my shoes won't chafe against the ankle. I can't keep the weight on anymore.

The rain has slackened off to a velvety dust by the time I get out. The city is so beautiful, veiled beneath another of these thousand persistent rains. The trees I walk under are an eye-aching green, the way they are at twilight. I love walking to work, even in bad weather, shuddering under low branches, ducking the heavens and measuring the trees against buildings, reckoning which are taller and more vulnerable.

I've been trained to look up. My favorite undergrad professor, Van Lare, always scolded us about missing the tops of buildings. "Glum youngsters!" he'd half rasp on walking lectures near campus. He was only about forty-five but his voice was already crypt-cold. "Look up, look up! Remember what Vitruvius said: We invented architecture because, unlike the beasts, we look up and have hands. Look there! See that? That is where our world meets the heavens." The heavens—always plural—were a favorite topic of Van Lare's. There was a time when I really tried to pay attention, when I entrusted myself to the heavens, looked up, oriented myself in relation to It All. But these days I keep my eyes at street level. I am content just to see where my feet will go next.

I wish my feet could take me away from work today, wish they could walk and keep walking. Today's rain is pleasant and invites you to play, nothing like the storms back home, that make you worry for the livestock outside town, calves spiraling into the mud and horses terrified under trees. It's true that if such a storm hits in the daytime, when the chickens are out, the ranchers will often find wet, dead ones after the clouds have passed over. Knowing no better, the birds tip their heads up to drink, or maybe to find an answer that will drown them for looking. Vitruvius was wrong: The beasts too can turn their faces to the sky. Lot of good it does them.

Rich and I live on 16th Street, the grandest and most traveled of the numbered streets in Northwest D.C. This is zero meridian for the United States, after all, anchored by the White House at its southern end, spooling into run-down mansions and minor embassies at our

1989

end. Until recently an old Victorian stood mothballed on the corner across from us, its arched front windows bricked in, iron porch leaning. A year ago, a lien notice was posted on the gate, then a For Sale sign. Last week a demolition crew put out orange cones in the street and surrounded the site with yellow tape. Rich and I drank a few bottles of wine on our porch over a week's time, watching the wrecking ball swing over the mansion's roof, reel up and crash down. On the third day the house fell in, spewing dust and sparks.

"Weird and beautiful," Rich said.

"Demolition puts on a better show than construction."

"I wonder what they're planning to build." He dropped the blind, shielding our room again from the bright worklight that flooded over the bed a moment before. "You know, I've been thinking about doing some things to our house. What would you say to that?"

I sat up. "You know what I would say."

"I don't know. I don't want to assume."

"What, you don't know—come on! I've said for years we ought to work on it. I've told you."

"Well, okay. So now I'm finally telling you."

It's sad to see the old mansion come down. I guess we both reacted to its destruction in different ways, but with similar results. Rich saw the possibilities for our real estate. I saw a chance to help our home avoid the other's doom. I had been hoping someone would come along to see the possibilities of the old place across from us as it was, to love it enough to take trouble for it. Obsolescence doesn't start with neglect, but rather with complacency. Someone sells or leaves behind a perfectly good house needing a few minor repairs, and the next thing you know it's a fixer-upper. From there it isn't a far trip to dereliction, abandonment, rot. The grander the place, the slower but harder it falls. Pretty soon it takes a designer's mind to see what it could be again. With luck a property like that is rescued, but more often it ends its days a gaping hole in the ground.

❋

Up the stone steps to my office, hello to our receptionist and the interns laboring at draft tables. A quick turn up the narrow service stair-

1989

case to the little office I share with Alice on the third floor. My boss, Meg, is sitting in my chair.

"Oh. Sorry I'm so late."

"No problem." She waves impatiently for me to come around to stand beside her. "Guess who wants us to hire him, bad?" She opens an unfamiliar portfolio on my drafting table, fanning out a few renderings with another firm's name on them. "Adam Schaeffer."

"Whoa. From Winston Charles Eckhart?"

"Yep. I think he was expecting to be made partner there this year, and now his nose is out of joint, and *we* could stand to profit. I couldn't believe he was for real when he called me, but I checked it out with some people, and he is definitely looking." She is looking too, looking hard at his drawings and site plans and sections and elevations, his after-photos and newspaper clippings: King's Crossroads office park (*New York Times*, *Architecture*, *Washington Post*); Newton, Illinois (*Chicago Tribune*, cover photo of a pull-out section entitled "Planning Where We Want to Go Home").

"We can't handle him. He's such a name."

"Why not? He still does the small stuff."

"Why would he want to?"

"Well, he wouldn't have to. He'd just go to conferences and parties and make people look at us. He wouldn't ever have to pick up a pencil again."

"Why wouldn't he want to?"

"He said he's tired of just designing things."

I'd like to be so tired. I move my old coffee cup, half full and growing mold spores, so I can lean in and pretend to consider the work more carefully. "Where would we even put him? I mean, did he see the offices? No offense."

Meg reshuffles the drawings to have another look. "I always find your honesty so bracing, David."

Let's start again. This is why I'm not partner, Rich has told me a thousand times. I'm not the sort to say the right thing under pressure, so I don't go to the conferences in Miami and Milan. I stay right here and assign tasks to the interns. "Okay, we could use someone who's as good at marketing as you," I say. "Really. I'm not just kissing ass."

18

1989

"I'd never accuse you of that, Dave, believe me."

"Who knows where the firm would go with someone like him, right?"

"Right. I was hoping you could take some guesses with me and him at a little informal meeting later this week. You know, talk through the possibilities."

I can't help but notice Alice hanging around just outside our door, hair damp from outside and briefcase still over her shoulder, trying to look busy at the fax while she waits for the right moment to come in. I wonder if Alice and her impeccable manners are also invited to this informal meeting. If Meg had asked me to close the door she wouldn't have put me in this position, but then again Meg wouldn't beat me out for any sensitivity awards. "I'd be honored. Delighted. I'd like that. That sounds great."

This is my other problem, the hemming and hawing when I am nervous or distracted. Henry calls it "rehearsing on stage." Meg stands up to go. "I had another piece of good news. Courtland Arms."

"Hey. They want us?"

"They want you in particular. They were so impressed with the way you handled the schedule for the Essex Apartments when it was in litigation all those months."

"Oh, wow. Wow."

"Second biggest project we've had since you got here. Congratulations. Can you get out there today to walk through it with the owner's rep?"

"Are you kidding? When?"

"Call her. Chloe's got the number."

Am I glad I didn't make a wisecrack about Schaeffer's Italian suits. Am I glad I'm in a new shirt. "I've got a visit out to Bethesda Towers at eleven, just for the sign-off."

"That can be couriered."

"No. Marge Quackenbos wants to draw out that last exquisite moment of torment. She loves me so."

"Well, we love her. We *love* her, David."

"Yes, yes. For three years, we have loved her, and we love her still. I will love her all the more when I don't have to see her ever again."

"Morning, David. Morning, Meg."

19

1989

"Alice." In she comes. It is her office too, of course. She leafs through Schaeffer's work, still on our drafting table. "Oh, whose are these?" As if she doesn't already know.

Meg lets Alice browse for a polite moment. "I was just telling David we might have a very bright young guy joining us soon."

"Wonderful."

Meg closes and zips the portfolio. "David, let me know about your schedule the rest of the week."

After Meg is gone, I speed-dial Rich at work. I hope he's at his desk. I want to share my pleasure and surprise about the new project. Already, though, the bloom is off it, and I wish Alice would find something to do, somewhere else to be, for just a few more minutes. I resent the stiff, studied way she sits at her desk, her back to me, going through the usual morning motions.

I get Rich's voice mail. "Honey, this is David. I've got good news. Meet me for lunch because I want to tell you in person. Okay?" I line up three pencils in front of me. "I'm going to Bethesda this morning, and then I need to be somewhere at two. Leave word on my voice mail where we can meet, and I'll pick up the message while I'm out."

Alice turns in her chair when I'm off the phone. She folds her hands between her thighs and smiles: a wide, fake, pep-squad smile. The smile my sister gives for photos and at moments when she's unhappy and wants you to know how brave she is. Jodie smiled like that when I chose an out-of-state college instead of following her to UT. She smiled that way at all the nurses and doctors who gave our mother such excellent care until her death two years ago, and she smiled like that when I told her about the HIV.

"Hey, that's great about the Courtland Arms, David."

"Isn't it?"

"Yep. I was going to ask if you were still free for lunch, but I guess you should go with Rich."

"Oh. Oh. Sorry, I forgot. Well, normally I'd say let's all go, the three of us. But I kind of want to . . ."

"Share all the good news. I know. Another time."

I glance at my watch. "Yes, good. Good. What do you have going tomorrow?"

20

1989

"Oh. This and that. Friday would be good."

Friday's too far away for me to tell. I nod anyway, grab my pencils and go.

Dust and garbage eddy up the escalator from the floor of the Metro, the wet wind lifting my jacket hem and gritting my eyes as I descend. The Metro always seemed so clean before I was diagnosed, but when your health is even a little precarious you notice the flotsam collecting in public corners. A woman at the foot of the moving steel stairs sings out, *Tha-a-ank you-ou-ou-ou, sweee-e-e-e-t Je-e-esus, my lo-o-o-ove,* blessing strangers who drop coins into her cup. It is her business to sing to Jesus and bless commuters, and she does it well. She makes me feel a little better, but I don't give her anything.

I've known Alice longer than anyone except my family and Henry. First she was my classmate at UVa Architecture, and now she's my office mate. She worked here for eighteen months before I did, in fact, and I suppose you could say she got me the job. She knew about the opening, recommended me, prepped me. That was a long time ago. In the years since, she has frequently lectured me about becoming a better team player. I imagine her drumming her fingers alone in our office right now, ruminating on what her team spirit got her this morning. In some ways she seems much younger than me, though we are virtually the same age. She still believes in fair play, in reaping rewards commensurate with effort. She believes in a safety net for those who struggle and mean well, despite the world's ample evidence to the contrary. In some ways I am grateful for her rock-solid faith in the Almighty Quid Pro Quo. I have made an effort on occasion to soak up her naïve and steady team spirit. She'd never stab me or anyone else in the back, never betray a colleague for her own sake. But I have seen this before, this vulnerability of hers, this capacity to feel wounded when she sees another person—let's put it bluntly, when she sees me—act efficiently on my own behalf, even when it doesn't directly affect her. Maybe it's one of those irreconcilable male-female differences. I feel guilty, and yet I have done nothing wrong. I was handed an opportunity. No, I earned it. I earned it. I took it. I did nothing wrong.

I really ought to give my sister a call tonight, to see how she's doing.

Up the first concrete block of Old Georgetown Road, a few little

1989

stores are shouting their last in the shadows of new office towers: LIQUIDATION. LOST OUR LEASE. EVERYTHING MUST GO. At the Bethesda Towers the building management company installed our scale model in the vast front lobby, which with its slanted atrium roof and transparent walls seems itself to be a gigantic display case.

I'm five minutes early, but Marge Quackenbos is tapping her nails on her glass-topped conference table anyway, as if I were fifteen minutes late. The table divides her neatly in the middle: chorus girl legs beneath the surface, and above the glass a face and hands tanned to the consistency of leather. She files her frosty nails to points, impudent and regal in her old-guard femininity, as her assistant and her lawyer look on.

From my dealings with her during the past three years I've learned how rude she is even when she intends to be polite. Her eastern Maryland straightness sometimes jackknifes into aggression. I imagine she hasn't always been accustomed to getting her way, but instead has climbed steadily on her excellent legs until she simply climbed higher than the boys. Sometimes when she turns her face just so, or if you manage to make her smile, you can catch the ghost of a little girl's face under the tanned folds, a girl who was proud and a little petty, never easily surprised but always willing to be deeply delighted. Now she is sitting at the top of her own Class A building, and she wants to know it's perfect in every respect, worth waiting for all these years.

"Look," she says. "What did your people tell you about the final weeks of construction?"

"Was there a problem?"

"The contractor billed a hell of a lot more than we agreed to. Have you used this guy before?"

"Numerous times. Let's see." I pull out the original work program and recent schedules. "The last weeks coincided with Easter or thereabouts, and there are probably holiday hours."

"Not eleven weeks worth of damn holidays," Marge's frosty lids drop over her eyes, lines rippling out when she squints at me.

"Weekends, night work... you had the April 30 completion date. As we discussed when we started, that's a tough date to meet even if the weather is with you, and this year it wasn't. There were two storms in February..."

"Let me see that." She won't wait for me to pass her the notebook. She pulls it out of my hands as soon as it's within her grasp and drags it to her over the wide, clear desk. "Jesus, they started pulling double shifts in March? Why?"

"Maybe they couldn't get all the workers they needed for earlier in the construction. Maybe a holdup on permitting somewhere. Sometimes there's a soil problem. I think I had a memo from the civil engineer... I sent it to you."

"I don't recall seeing it."

Well, what a surprise. "The problems are often interlocking toward the end of a big project. We could sit here all day untangling them if you insist, but I think we ought to declare victory because the building is completed, close to budget even after three years—"

Marge has stopped listening. "What's this maybe stuff? Maybe this, maybe that... don't you know? You're the project architect."

"Eleven weeks' overtime for a long, large project isn't unheard of, and it's not half bad."

Meg, if she were here, would be pushing the final paperwork under the client's nose, but I'm not Meg. I wait, watching the lawyer pore over the program notebook as if it will yield greater secrets.

Marge just looks at me across her desk, both of us reflected grimly in the glass. She raises her brows and lifts her chin, waiting. I don't know if I'm being invited to explain further, or if she is thinking and just happens to have rested her eyes where I occupy space.

"I believe what my client is asking you for is a little extra assurance that the work wasn't rushed." The lawyer's not looking at his watch, I notice. He has all day, too, and for him it's billable time. "What if you fax us the missing memo and we'll get back to you?"

"What if I fax you the missing memo and you simply sign off? The work is done. We are sitting in it."

"Yes, and a year from now if a pipe bursts or a window blows out in a storm, where will you be?"

"It depends on how the year goes." Oh. There I go again, the man so far from being partner material, the player who grabs the ball from his

1989

teammate before he knows where he's headed: straight into the end zone, alone. "I think you'll find over time that this place is solid construction and wears well. But you're right to be cautious, of course. Send your approval by certified mail, if you would. I wouldn't want to lose it." I retrieve my work program from Marge's chilly hand. I'm sorry Meg wasn't here to help me avoid this incomplete approval, but glad she missed more proof of my ineptness with this sort of thing. Marge escorts me from her office and gestures into the space beyond her suite. "I guess I don't have to show you the way out," she says. "Since you designed it, right?" She turns on her heel with a deeply delighted, unsurprised laugh.

※

I'm late to meet Rich. "I ordered for us already," he says. "I have a lot to do before I head to the airport."

"The airport?"

"You didn't forget, did you?"

"I didn't forget. Rich, I *didn't.*"

"All right, you didn't."

"Seattle. Right? You're giving a talk—"

"Yes. On . . . ?"

"Pacific Rim stuff. Family farming."

"Family entrepreneurship. But close enough."

The waiter puts our plates down: fish for me. Rich butters his bread, takes a bite, and butters it again near the spot he just ate from, then puts the knife we share back on the butter plate. I take a deep breath, trying to remember the little things don't matter. *Don't start, David. Be nice. Look at the shadows under his eyes. Because of you he loses sleep at night.*

"Seattle's going to be a bitch," he says. "I wish they'd quit scheduling these trips at the last minute so I could skip the weekend stayovers."

I try not to picture him on Saturday night in some restaurant like this, morose, by himself. Or worse, going out to the bars. Rich is beyond discreet, though. He'd never fool around on a business trip.

"What's your mysterious good news?" he asks.

I fork up some salmon to please him, though I am not hungry. "Meg handed me a big project this morning. An apartment complex in Adams Morgan. Historic rehab."

"David! That's great. When do you start work?"

"Today. This afternoon. Come with me on the walk-through."

"Wouldn't that look unprofessional?"

"How? You clean up nice. You're wearing a suit."

"Anyway, I can't. I have a stack of stuff to get through before I leave."

I push my plate across to him. "Does this seem dry to you?"

"A little."

I signal the waiter and order a salad. Normally I don't order anything uncooked in front of Rich. He raises his brows after the waiter goes. "Look, I'm sorry," I tell him. "I feel like living dangerously today."

"I didn't say anything."

We spend the rest of the meal in near silence. I guess we're entering another phase of tension. Until recently we managed pretty well to sidestep bad moments, but more and more lately it's like trying to take a shortcut in a city you don't know as well as you thought. Every switchback and side street takes you to another point in the same tangle.

"I've got to get back." Rich snaps his credit card down on the table between us.

"I've got this, please. I invited you."

"It's all right, David. Let me pick this up."

"Fine, then. Thank you." I bring the last two words up as unreluctantly as I can and open my hand to take his. "I'm going to miss you this weekend."

He smiles tightly, glances around, then touches his fingertips to mine—his tenuous public caress, primed for retraction.

"It's a hand, Rich, come on. Take it. I don't think it's covered under the sodomy statute."

He doesn't like this. He never likes it when I do this in public. He takes my hand in a vise grip.

"All right, David? Here, here's my whole hand. All right?"

To my surprise, his eyes well up with tears. The check comes. "Sorry," he tells me. "I need to borrow my hand back so I can pay."

25

# 1989

An electric fan ticks back and forth in the lobby hearth of the Courtland Arms in counterpoint to the tock, tock, tock of the big clock on the wall. I've been sitting for a half hour, if the clock is right. I keep forgetting my watch. The filmy, damp light of the humid afternoon shines in through the front windows, crossing the floor along the worn footpaths to the elevators. Soot and years of tracked-in soil blur the edges of the floor mosaic, black on white in a diaperwork pattern.

My head hurts.

I have the lobby to myself while I wait for the owner's rep. It all seems as though it could never change: the dead mechanical fire and the cheap fan in front of it, the whirring metronome of the electric clock, the ancient floor. I jump up to open the door for a bent woman struggling in with her groceries. A pink straw-brimmed hat shades her thin face. Does she know what is going to happen here? Does she have someplace to go? She thanks me for opening the door.

I sit back in my overstuffed armchair, crossing my legs and swinging the top foot in time with the clock, but its rhythm overtakes mine or falls behind, depending on which way you choose to listen. The ventilation in this lobby is abysmal. A key turns in the lock of the front door, and warm air rolls in from the street.

"David? Marcia Zenk. How are you?" She pushes a strand of dark hair back from her forehead. She seems too young. I search for signs of incipient ruin in her face, hoping I'm dealing with something of a peer. Yes, just the shadow of a jowl beginning, a few lines in the neck where it peeks out of the navy sweater. She is at least thirty, I hope.

"Look, I'm in a bit of a bind," she says. "I hope we can show you what you need to see by three-thirty, because I'm committed to be across town soon."

"I have to be somewhere myself," I lie diplomatically, automatically. She walks me to the elevator and punches the button for up. "We'll look at the top floor and the second and I'll show you the four different layouts. You've got an easy job on this place, I think."

"Oh, I can tell already it's a solid property." The elevator is freshly

1989

painted a thick coat of cream over years and layers of more offending shades.

"There's paneling under here." Marcia indicates the walls of the elevator. "And under that—"

"Who knows? Are these the original elevators?"

She nods. "So there's almost certainly nothing in it worth saving," I say. "I mean, the mechanism will have to be replaced, so why not change the carriage too? What do the owners want to do with the lobby?"

"More like, what do they want to spend?" Marcia says. "Did you have something specific in mind?"

I hedge. "This building was built around 1920?"

"Right. The owners want a more contemporary feel. You know, something warm and bricky. So like, we could have a wood look in the elevator. And probably wall-to-wall carpet in the halls. Or fabric walls. Do you like that sort of watered-silk pattern they have sometimes in wallpapers?"

"That's not my call," I say pointedly. If she doesn't want to do the building justice, I can't be bothered with recommending fabric swatches. The elevator doors release us into a dim hallway with worn carpet and doors of deep blue. Another long, gloomy corridor about which I can do little.

"New lighting will help." I am trying to be nice.

"You think?" Marcia's brow wrinkles. "Wouldn't just putting in more fluorescents be okay?"

"Halogen's cheaper in the long run." Her owners could probably care less about the long run. They'll turn this place over in ten years.

She opens apartment 912 and lets me in ahead of her. "I read somewhere that halogen exposure might cause cancer."

"If you don't filter it properly. You just need little halogen condoms, that's all." I turn in place in the small living room. "Life's short. It might as well be pretty."

She laughs uncertainly. She isn't yet thirty, I decide.

The living room is too warm in the afternoon light. I open the windows there and in the bedroom, but I can't get a breath of air. The

1989

cross-ventilation is not what it should be for a building this age. Sloppy design. The corners of the walls are blunted and the ceiling is cracking in plaster blossoms that shower debris onto the empty floor. I have to duck going through the door to the dressing area, another sloppy touch. It's all unremarkable except for a few failsafe details of the era: the ornamental radiator almost hidden by a metal cage, the amulet drains in the bath and sink. And in the main room, a dogtooth frieze around the damaged ceiling.

Marcia points. "We'd like to get rid of that wall and open up the foyer."

"Mmm-hmm. Had any luck finding the original plans?" My dead predecessor's choices will constrain me, and he doesn't seem to have been a meticulous man.

"We're tracing them. We're trying." From the offhand delivery, I can tell that they're hoping I'll just make do.

"I know an excellent research firm," I offer. "You really, really need to know what you are starting with."

"Oh, of course."

I can tell, even without my watch, that three-thirty has arrived. I know because I am losing strength. "I guess we can call it a day, for today. Let me go back and put some ideas on paper for you. We shouldn't rush this part."

Marcia agrees. I go home to sleep.

But when I get home, a second wind picks me up and deposits me at the kitchen table, where I sketch a quick plan for our house on the back of a phone pad. First and foremost, a sunroom with a steep glass roof, copper flashing that will go verdigris over time, to match the little fauns and figures that populate our back garden. An oval skylight in the bedroom, a bigger bathroom with an open wardrobe, paneled in bleached pine. I list the things to be corrected along the way: replace windows, repoint the bricks in the façade, and maybe even get a better heating and cooling system as long as we're opening walls.

The warmth outside our window is deceptive. It's late September already, the days will be cold soon, and construction season will end. Most of the rubble from the old house across the street has been cleared away, and a sparse crop of weed trees is already above ground. Ailanthus—Tree of Heaven—it grows so fast.

1989

I put down my pencil, stretch my back against my chair, dial Rich at work.

"Hi."

"Hi. How did your walk-through go?"

"I came home early."

I sense the little catch in his voice before he speaks. "You okay?" he asks.

"Fine. I just had so little time left in the day, and it's gotten nice outside. I wanted to be home. I miss you already."

"Likewise."

"I'm sorry about lunch today. You know I love you."

A little silence, as he tries to frame a response that is appropriate from his desk at work. "It's okay if you can't talk," I say.

"I can talk. Give me a minute. It just seems like you always want . . . the one thing I haven't thought to offer you. And you ignore what I do offer you."

"Okay." I pull the list of improvements away from the phone pad and start a fresh sheet, a drawing this time. "I'm listening."

"That's all," he says. I could put the solarium where the old kitchen porch is now. It doesn't have to be very big if the ceiling goes the full height of the house.

"What are you doing?" he asks suspiciously.

"Planning our new house. Want a sunroom?"

"Sure. I'd like a bath with a view, too."

"You got it. At least on paper. I'll see you Tuesday, okay? I love you."

"Same here."

"I mean it."

"So do I."

I fix tea and bring it up to bed, settling in to draw in the half-light of evening, my pencil scratching out the precise geometry of wishes. Because it's Friday, an old urge rises in me as the light fails: to put down my pen and stop making marks until nightfall tomorrow, as was the rule in my house growing up. Soon, if my mother were alive, if that household I grew up in were still intact, I would freshen up and go downstairs to join Jodie and my parents at the table for chicken and rice, and fruit with kosher Jell-O for dessert, with its disconcerting

29

1989

aftertaste, like the scent of ivy. It's said that nightfall brings an added soul to the house where Shabbat is kept. I used to think that was why my mother hid her eyes when she lit the candles, because she was afraid of the extra soul the house inhaled with darkness. Now I put down my pencil, but only for a moment, to rub my forehead in a parody of that devout gesture. I plan to keep working through Sabbath. I don't have a day each week to spare anymore, even for an additional soul.

Besides, there's no extra soul in my house tonight. Only the silence of Rich's absence, so unaccustomed that it seems a presence. It drifts upstairs and winds itself around me, chilling me under the blankets.

"You shouldn't worry so much about him," says my friend Henry. I'm sitting in his new apartment a few blocks from our place, the second floor of a turreted neo-Gothic on Florida Avenue. His living room is round. "He shouldn't worry so much about you either. Do you know he called me last night to check on you?"

"No way."

"Yes way. He tried to make me think he was just calling to see how I was. Like he does that on a regular basis." One of Henry's main beefs since Rich and I got together is that Rich suddenly made me the social secretary for both friendships.

"I'm jealous of this layout," I say. "I always wanted a round living room. Not efficient, but so interesting."

"Oh please," says Henry. "If you'd stayed with me, you'd have one now." He's been given to these flirtatious little stabs ever since he got back from the West Coast, as if our history together were more illicit and ornate than it is. We were roommates in college, roommates after. Except for an odd careless night here and there, that was all.

Oh please. Henry was always the last in our group of friends to embrace current phrases. He took it as a point of pride. When he finally decides to use these expressions, he does it with a kind of reluctance, a delivery so flat it seems begrudging.

"Anyway," he continues, "you and Rich are now intertwined in a typical dance of regret. He needs you to make him feel bad, and you need him to make you feel bad."

1989

"That's not funny."

"Who's being funny?" Henry considers himself an astute judge of character, like most professional loners. For years he's gone from one terrific job in one great city to the next even better one. He could fill a room with people who think he's wonderful, but I may be his only real friend. This tone of authority he takes on a dizzying range of subjects does put people off, but I suspect he's also choosing to do a little dance all his own, a kind of frenetic Watusi like his trademark dance when we were boys going to clubs together. Always he'd find the high spot on the dance floor, maybe the bare riser reserved for the drag show or even, a few times, the vacated perch of a cage dancer on break. There he could see and be seen without ever rubbing up against a stranger.

It's not fastidiousness. Henry doesn't have such an exacting nature, though you'd never know it by looking around right now. The apartment is bare except for a chrome and red Formica table and chairs in the kitchen, a futon on a cheap frame, and a small black desk with a laptop, its screensaver scattering stars. "Where's all your stuff, Henry?"

"Left it in LA. My brother took a lot of it."

"You could get new furniture, you know. They have stores here and everything."

"I will give that some serious thought. Now, you know what I want to do right now? I mean right now?"

"What?"

"I want to improve our minds. There's this amazing folk-art installation downtown at the Museum of American Art; it's called the Throne of Heaven. I think you'd get into it."

"It's Saturday. All those tourists."

"Since when do you hate a crowd?"

Since I don't know what other people might be carrying, that's when. I don't discuss or indulge my hesitation further, though. We go by Metro to Gallery Place, where the museum sits up to its marble petticoats in bombed-out neighboring buildings. The developers are just sitting on this area, waiting for the city to cave in further. Something will finally happen here someday, for better or worse. There is talk, there are plans. Restaurants and theaters and first-tier art spaces,

1989

decent housing or hotels and high-priced apartments. Meanwhile, the old businesses barely hang on.

Naturally the Metro's escalator is stalled. As we climb the metal steps, I feel as if the air is thinning. I'm so winded I have to stop partway. There is a feeling like lead in my chest—molten, earthbound, and sour. Henry waits at the top for me to catch up, and when I do he slows his steps but doesn't dare, not yet, to take my elbow.

"I'm okay," I lie.

He is kind. He pretends nothing is happening. He pushes on, slowly, letting me catch my breath. "Throne of Heaven was this labor of love, this utterly crazy piece of work that a government janitor perfected in his spare time," he explains. "He worked on it for fourteen years. The only reason he stopped is that he died. I mean he rented a special space to build it in and everything. It was his passion. Here, it's just inside, on your left."

Set back in a dark alcove, James Hampton's tribute to God is not a throne, but a throne room, a holy gathering place of shimmering discards—foil-covered cardboard, and dead lightbulbs also encased in foil, once-violet paper crowns faded to a rich sepia, placards covered with the weird, fluid script the angels are said to have revealed to Hampton in dreams. Elaborate golden and silver wings break out from every plane. Two words are inscribed in English atop the central throne: FEAR NOT. Under the exhibit lights, the great throne gives off a borrowed shimmer, like a moon.

A black-and-white photograph behind glass shows Hampton posing stiffly in his garage. His round spectacles reflect the camera flash. He stands without expression with his back to the throne, as if oblivious to his own creation.

I can see why Henry wanted to bring me. Old friend, it moves me that he knows what I will like. James Hampton was possibly crazy, and certainly steeped in fundamentalist hokum like so many people I avoided when I was growing up. His vision of heaven is not like mine—his heaven is a celestial living room; mine is a broad sunny plain in which pure thought is action, movement effortless, connection continuous with a core of energy that enlivens and enriches— what?—whatever. I can't picture such energy having presence in any

1989

ordinary sense of the word or needing a place to sit down. Presence would be all there is, nothing standing inside or outside it. I want to be lost in a blinding big yes like that, such a subsuming light. What good is consciousness without experience? What is experience but the sensual net of the body? With no body, I want no consciousness. With no body, I want to be nothing anymore, and I want to reconnect with everything.

"What are you thinking?" Henry's touch on my arm is light but sure.

"Wondering how the core of the knowable universe can fit on a throne."

"Well, how many angels can dance on the head of a pin?"

"A little too symmetrical for my taste," I complain, but secretly I am enchanted by this little glimpse of divinity conceived at human scale. So what if Hampton was an ecstatic fundamentalist, a literalist with an active dream life? He was also an elegant architectural thinker. He's built an enclosed universe, like one of those gardens inside a Fabergé egg: cramped and contained, yet suggesting infinity. More like a hall of mirrors, come to think of it, reflecting and reflecting and reflecting with an unrelenting reciprocity that causes claustrophobia and vertigo at one shot. It isn't so much that a god will ever sit there. I don't think that was Hampton's point. It seems he was dogged to complete the crude spatial expression of the boundless, the application of found materials to finite surfaces in rendering his vision of eternity.

Henry walks me partway back to my place afterward. He gives me an awkward peck in front of the Masonic Temple, where we used to sunbathe between the sphinxes' paws, when we first moved to D.C. and lived together off 18th Street. "I'm so glad I'm home, David," he says. "I'm so glad to be near you again." And then he throws his arms around me, holds me tight until I break free as gently as I can.

It's a warm fall day, not quite windless. Maybe the slant of autumn light suggested my idea of heaven back in the museum, that dazzling bright plain. It's an unusually sunny vision for me. It's more like something my mother might see, she who kept separate dishes and listened patiently with hands folded in synagogue, never swaying and murmuring on her feet, as my father did, except when it was utterly called for, during the Amidah or when someone in the family had recently

33

1989

died and Kaddish was appropriate. Underneath the primly buttoned cardigans she wore to shul through the icy air-conditioning of summer and the drafty, inadequate insulation against winter, she nurtured a pagan's wild warm heart, her primly folded hands cradling a truth more elemental and ancient than even Judaism admits. My mother's explanation of creation, first offered me when I was four or so, was that God imbued the light and wind with their powers, and that the way trees move was the constant proof of God's constant presence. She was fond of pointing out the many storms and floods of Genesis, the winds stated and implied in the appearance of the burning bush, in the restless angels that climbed up and down the ladder of Jacob's vision, the parting of the waters after Exodus—how else were these things made possible except through the awesome power of wind and light?

I think for my mother these were relatively simple explanations to get a small child started in the struggle to understand life. But for me these theories suggested a complexity lurking beneath the ordinary, tree-lined neighborhood and shaded back garden that were my first habitat. It has always seemed to me that my mom's theory of the heavens has the same elegance and mystery as the "simple" state of being Tibetan Buddhists call ground luminosity: the first and returning point of creation before consciousness.

Because I take my time going home—I have to keep stopping to get my breath—I see what she is talking about now, finally, clearly. The trees are lively with a life not only their own. The warmth of the sun is a creaturely presence; the barely perceptible movement of the wind, a force in equal parts palpable and subtle. To be always there, so ubiquitous as to be forgotten and taken for granted: is there no greater demonstration of a creator's love than that? My mother would call it proof of love, anyway. For her it was simple: Presence equals love. For me it was simple, too. Throughout childhood, I was alone underfoot in the kitchen as she talked on the phone while setting the table, doing the breakfast dishes, and getting out a cold lunch for us even as she started the evening dinner. Her presence was my world, her scent and nearness as she moved through the bright patches of window light, chatting into the receiver, laughing, writing down notes to herself, were my assurance that all was well. These endless phone conversations somehow reassured me. I knew the telephone was my mother's link to the outside world, the spiraling beige cord an umbilicus that swung and arced behind her from sink to refrigerator to stove and back again. Her women friends were also home all day with children, also members of committees for the League of Women Voters, Hadassah, PTA, March of Dimes. My sister was most of the day at school, and my father was all day at work, until night fell. The daytime house hummed with the work of appliances, and my mother—my creator—spun out endless plans on the phone for tomorrow and next week and the week after. I felt as safe as I ever have.

One night I was certain I felt God in the forced darkness of the room Jodie and I shared at night, the dense velvet so opulent and oppressive in the summer heat that I felt overwhelmed and terrified by a presence of extraordinary force.

I struggled with my sister over control of the lamp. I remember the heft of her arms and upper body as she leaned on me, triumphant, to plunge us back into darkness. We still lived in the little house near the airport, with only two bedrooms and one bathroom. There was no place for me to go for light except the living room, which meant a treacherous journey down the long, scary hallway with its dark oil paintings (products of my father's shutting himself away each Sunday in the garage). When she'd had enough of my sniffling, we made an uneasy compromise, and Jodie let me sleep with her in the dark. To my shame I wet the bed a few hours later. She shook me awake and pushed me to the floor. Silent, grim mouthed, and resigned to her fate as the eldest, she shushed my crying with the offer of her hand and made me come with her to fetch towels from the bathroom. After we blotted the accident as best we could, she sequestered herself in my dry bed. Without a word to me, she clicked the night light on, turned away, and pulled the covers over her head.

❋

Walking pneumonia sounds almost cheerful, like Waltzing Matilda. Like, *oh it's nothing, a touch of walking pneumonia.* It sounds comical, zany, something you might call a friend: He's a stitch, a card, a case of the walking pneumonia. This is my first time with a new doctor, Dr.

1989

Lerner. After I've submitted to the whole charmless routine—weight, blood pressure, interview with an intern—I'm left alone in a narrow, blank exam room to remove my shirt and wait for a knock at the door.

"David Baum." Dr. Lerner, a little stooped and smoothly bald, says my name like an oath. "Mr. Baum, it's my pleasure to examine you today." He listens, looks, and prods, then sits back on his exam stool, rolling around on his heels so suddenly I think he'll smack the wall. "Well. Your throat is pretty red."

He sounds impressed, so I try to look suitably alarmed.

"It's hard to know much until we get the culture and your T4-cell count back, but it seems likely that we'll need to be watching for yeast outbreaks, okay? I'm prescribing a Mycelex troche for the throat. Now, this could be PCP, which is treatable but no fun. My guess is it's probably just regular, old-fashioned walking pneumonia. Ever had that as a kid?"

"Never. I've always been pretty healthy."

"Well, good. Your natural immunity is an ally. Have you ever taken Bactrim, David? Take it every day for the next seven to ten—call me at the end of the week, let me know how you are. Meanwhile, if I get back the culture tomorrow and it's PCP or some rare tropical disease, I'll call you to work on Plan B. But Bactrim is very effective, has a nice broad spectrum. Once we get you back in shape it will be part of the routine, three times a week from now on. Right? How long have you been on AZT?"

"I'm not."

"You're not?"

"No. Not now. I took it for a while some years ago. All it did was make me sick."

"Well. All in the balance of risks, right? Now we are at that point where the risk of serious illness is greater, yes? So we'll start back on the AZT, and you need to get some iron supplement to go with that." He hands me another prescription. "Okay, what else is going on for you? How is your hearing? Any sudden rashes? Loss of appetite?"

Don't blame me for saying nothing, with this guy still wielding his blank prescription pad. "I'll need to get blood work to test for antibodies to a very common virus among the general population, not just people with AIDS," he continues. "We can do that when you come in for follow-up, since you're feeling so crummy, but I don't want to put it off too long. You want to hear about that now? It's not an active infection, just something to watch. You have something like a thirty percent chance of carrying it."

"It's that eye disease, right? My old doctor tested me for it. He said I have it."

Lerner gives me a look. "You have it or you have the antibody for it?"

"I have the antibody, I guess. I mean, it's not active."

"How long ago was this?"

"I really can't remember. About a year."

"David, I'm glad you came to me when you did. AIDS is a management problem as much as anything. We have lots of answers now, but a lot of those answers have to come from you, right? We're a team. If you play for me, I play for you." Lerner smiles and lifts his brows, just like my dad teaching us to swim, urging us to the deep end alone. "Let's talk about following up at the end of this month and focusing on a new CMV scan and some other housekeeping chores. So. Bet you'd like to get dressed and go home, wouldn't you?"

"That's it?"

"For now. See you at the end of the month."

I don't panic until I'm in the lobby, then I call Henry at his office to come get me and the car. "I'm sorry," I explain. "Rich isn't back till tomorrow, and I've felt shitty all weekend. Can you just come get me? Can you stay?" I've put off dread all weekend, and it's exhausting, just how exhausting I haven't wanted to face until I had to. Henry is there in the promised half hour. He takes my keys, takes my hand, and leads me to a warm stone bench in the water garden outside the hospital. I watch the koi lumber and twist in the fish pond as other outpatients, some of them lame, some of them hale, some of them aged, pass in and out of the sliding glass doors with a breath of cool air at each entry and exit. Henry is there in the turnaround, driving my car, and he is here at my elbow, his touch just what's needed, neither insulting nor uncaring. It's absurd to think he can save me the trouble of dying, as absurd as my thinking I can spare him the trouble of losing another friend. But at the moment I am satisfied to know that, now the time has come to

1989

call a friend, I have somehow had the good sense or good fortune to have the right kind of friend.

At home I fall onto the couch for a compromised nap. When I wake up an hour later feeling sticky and unsatisfied, I hear Henry in the dining room, moving things off the table: keys, unwashed glasses and bowls, mail I haven't bothered to open, put-off magazines and newspapers. He pads to the edge of the couch and leans over me, smiling, silent. I stare back until I make him look away. He smooths his neck with his hand, capturing the loose skin under his jaw between thumb and forefinger, then looks back at me again.

"You're an angel, and I'm a wreck," I say. "I don't deserve a friend like you."

"You're all right. Feel like eating something?"

"I could."

"Come on then."

He serves me a simple meal of buttered noodles and peas, then hands me the phone to dial Rich's room in Seattle. "It's only five-thirty there," he says. "A good time to call the hotel." Sure enough, Rich answers on the third ring. Our conversation is efficient, unsurprising. It's a call we've both awaited with little pleasure for the past three years. I tell him I am sick, that Henry will stay the night with me, and I ask if he can skip tomorrow's meetings and come home early. He says he absolutely will. He always knew one day he would have to.

※

Rich got home, jet-lagged and beside himself, at two this afternoon. Now Henry is making tonight's dinner while Rich sets the table for three. Rich had barely dropped his luggage in the doorway before he flung himself into action. He lined up all my new medicines in the door of the fridge and made a list of what gets taken when. This is posted in the kitchen now, among the photos of friends and family, blocking the cartoons and postcards and funny magnets we have collected over the years. He sat down to his PC and updated our list of important phone numbers to include the new doctor, the local AIDS information hotline, my insurance group and member numbers, and a twenty-four-hour telephone number to call for preapproval of a

1989

hospital stay. "We're in this together," he says. I wish he would sit down for a few minutes.

After dinner Henry does the dishes discreetly and leaves us. I punch my sister's number into the phone, rubbing my eyes until sworls of light appear. While I wait for her to answer I play with the pen Rich has brought me as a souvenir. The working half of the barrel is red, the top is clear and filled with water, with a little boat that fits neatly into its ferry slip, then travels away when you tip the pen the other way. Jodie answers when I have just tipped the pen back, and the boat nestles into its slip just so.

"Hi, it's David."

"Buster! Where've you been? I must have called you four times this weekend."

"I'm sorry I haven't called."

"Just don't do that again. You scare me. I'm sorry, but you do when you disappear like that. Everything okay? How's work? How's the house going?"

"Fine. We haven't really started yet. I'm—"

"Hang on a sec. Gina, put that down! Put it back where you found it. No, I said. Listen, Buster, I'm glad you called because I wanted to talk about Dad's birthday present."

I up-end the pen, and the boat slides out of its berth. "Jodie. Before we get into that—"

"What? What's wrong? What happened?"

"Nothing happened. Everything is fine. I have a little flu."

"Oh. God." She lets out a breath, like a sigh of relief. "You want me to tell Dad?"

"It's flu, Jodie. You could get flu. Rich could get flu. You know, normal people."

"Don't."

"Sorry." I tip the pen again. "I'll tell him next time I call him. I will. I'd like to be in good health when we talk about, you know. The whole thing."

Gina chants in the background, "Hi Uncle Buster Hi Uncle Buster Hi Uncle Buster."

"Gina, hush! Put that back, I said." A slap and my name rises into a

39

1989

wail, interspersed with hiccups. "David, how long are you going to put this off, already?"

"Jodie, do you want to call me later instead of hitting your kid?"

"Nice try, David. Gina's fine. We are talking about you." The wailing dies down. Maybe Gina has run into the next room or been invited to her mother's lap.

"Look. I'm sorry. I don't want to get into this now."

Jodie will probably cry a little after she hangs up, sitting on her bright linoleum floor and trying to explain to Gina why Mommy gets so sad sometimes. "No, I'm sorry, David. I didn't mean to be so harsh, what I said. I'm sorry."

"Well. I think we've established that everybody's sorry." From the kitchen doorway, Rich signals with an imaginary cup to his lips, saucer in his palm: *Coffee?* I nod.

"It's just a little bug," I reassure my sister. "If I'd gotten my shot for the season like I was supposed to, I'd be as healthy as the next guy. About Dad's present?"

"It seems silly now."

"No, let's talk about it."

"Well. It's nothing, really. I just saw one of those things at Brookstone, where you can carry a beeper on your key chain and find your car in the parking lot."

Our father spends a lot of time in parking lots, strolling through the great rectangle of asphalt that serves the mall or grocery store or the apartment complex where he picks up the woman he takes out now and then. The Lincolns and Chryslers in silvers and blues line up neatly in their allotted spaces. In this gleaming sea of metal I can see him activating the key chain. Safely, in orderly fashion, he is led by invisible sound waves to the door of his car. It has an infrared pinlight so he can see his lock in the dark.

"That sounds fine."

"Not too gimmicky?"

"No. Just fine. How much do I owe you?"

"About thirteen dollars. Shouldn't we get him something else?"

"No."

"Are you all right, really?"

1989

I just want my damn coffee and to get off the phone. "Yes, sure," I lie. Maybe I'd rather have Rich bring me scotch. I'd like to lie on our kitchen floor the way I did as a kid, listening to the refrigerator thrum and watching my mom's bare feet kiss the linoleum with little smacks as she moved from stove to sink. Sometimes when she shifted her weight or turned, her thigh bone adjusted in its socket with a satisfying click. I want such perfect, solemn pleasures returned to me, to watch others play out the mysteries of adulthood and to be the one who is safe. I am not just thinking about any cup of coffee now, or scotch any old way. I want the perfect temperature and strength. I want it neat.

"David?"

"I'm tired a lot. That's about it."

"I can't believe it's happening."

"Nothing is happening. Nothing is happening. Would you put Gina on so I can say hi?"

"Sure."

"Hi, Uncle Buster."

"Hi, Pepper. What did you do today?"

"We made a bean casserole."

"Mmm."

"I grew a bean in my class, and we put it in there."

"What kind of bean?"

"A green one."

"You grew a green bean? Did you eat it? Did it taste good?"

Silence. Jodie's voice: "Tell Uncle David goodbye."

"It was mushed up in there. A casserole gets cheese in it."

Jodie: "Okay, that's enough, you're using up long distance. Tell Uncle David goodbye."

"Goodbye." The receiver drops and misses its mark, then is replaced, severing the connection.

❋

After the demolition, there is no more activity on the site across the street until the end of September. I can't tell if it's related, but city trucks pull up one day and begin excavating the water main at our corner. They stop as mysteriously as they started, the work half finished,

41

1989

the pipe exposed in its bed of pink sand, a pile of concrete sherds beside it. From a poorly resealed joint, a rivulet of water trickles down the street for days, wetting the bright leaves, newly fallen.

In the evening Rich and sometimes Henry and I take advantage of the waning good weather, strolling over to 17th Street for drinks or dinner. The sidewalks are stamped with messages in Day-Glo paint: You Are Here, We Are Everywhere. SILENCE = DEATH. ACTION = LIFE. The Gay mandala, a pink triangle in a circle, with the command: QUEERS BASH BACK.

Some days I want the house to myself, or Rich does. This isn't new. What's new is the careful way we each ask the other for some "private time," the cautious feints we make to clear a space in the other one's schedule, not to be together, but to be apart. One Saturday, Rich makes it clear that he thinks it's his turn today. I've been around a lot this past week, home from work again, prone on the sofa in my socks for hours, immovable and exhausted the first day, depressed and silent the next. I set myself a deadline that second day, to be off the couch and moving, to be at least presentable in jeans and T-shirt by the time Rich got home. I fell asleep and woke up to see him standing over me, concerned, irritable, smelling of car exhaust and the light sweat of the office worker after a long day. "Are you okay, really?" he asked. It sounded, somehow, like an accusation.

Saturday I am fortunately better, well enough to consider a long walk, with the weather's cooperation. The sun gives off the crisp, bittersweet light of early October. I'll go downtown, maybe to the river. I stop at a coffee place along the way to pick up lunch. For a moment I consider calling Henry or another friend, but after a block or two I start to feel confident and contented on my own, in a way that I just now realize has become unfamiliar.

I won't stop along the way or take the bus. I'm interested in moving my body today, feeling the relative health and competency of my limbs. I choose as many side streets as I can, focusing far into the distance to appreciate the elegant allées of autumn leaves, bright branches arching over my head like the ceiling of a cathedral.

I used to drive and drive when I came here, partly to learn the area, but also to see what it would take for me to run out of road, to move

42

1989

through the city until something showed me I had no place else to go. I never went quite far enough to run out of road, though I went halfway to New York once, in the middle of the night, drunk, with my then-boyfriend of the moment, Henry and Alice and her boyfriend Joe asleep on top of each other in the back like a trio of kittens. Every trip, even that one, landed me back at my own empty bed.

There's quite a commotion as I approach downtown. Helicopters chop up the bluish air over the pit carved out on Pennsylvania Avenue where the final building of the Federal Triangle is going up. Hundreds of people circle its rim, holding their cameras in front of them for proof that a hole that big can be opened in the earth and nothing around it seem touched. I think at first that something must have happened at the site, but then I see that these viewers are only part of a general movement down the avenue. Then I am in it, with hundreds of people pushing past me. Instinctively I cover my mouth and nose, seeking a space apart from the crush of pedestrians. It's like that classic film fragment the news channels and documentaries show for Crowded New York City: humanity marching tenfold abreast as oblivious but related as ants. As I begin to focus, I notice something unusual: a lot of the people around me are men. A lot of these men are traveling with the aid of a friend or a crutch or even, in a couple of cases, in wheelchairs. They are suspiciously thin-haired, not in an ordinary way, but with patchy hair that looks like new-hatched feathers. Now I cover my mouth and nose in earnest. These are my fellows, I am sure. AIDS cases. We are indeed everywhere.

I had to have read it in the paper or heard about it from friends. How could I have forgotten? Just when I was most anxious to be alone, I've walked into the goddamned sanctimonious AIDS Quilt.

I wait for the stoplight to go green so I can cross. The sky sheds a filtered light that saturates colors. Across the street, the people seated in clumps under trees are like animated dabs. Two children turn somersaults in the grass. A slender man carries a red rose. A little girl with straight brown hair and a yellow raincoat follows the sound of her mother's call. I choose a path away from them all, up the hill to the Washington Monument. A knot of people gathers to look down at all the rest.

1989

Several plain trucks are parked in a circle around a soundstage hung with brightly colored patches. A woman's voice recites the names of the dead. She is close to the beginning: Lovely Mark Anderson, Gary Anson, David Applebaum . . .

I get a chill hearing two names back to back, a familiar one with one so like my own. I knew a Gary Anderson back in Texas, or was it Anson? He was a shy boy I went to school with, very pretty, with a high blush in his cheeks and bright green eyes.

Instead of the smooth expanse of quilt I expected, the lawn is dotted with individual pillows of plastic. A drop of rain pings against my shoulder. The voice stops the recitation abruptly. "By now the quilts should be in plastic. Those of you who drove down with trucks, please come around as we discussed on Friday for the rain plan." The voice then resumes its funereal roll. The crowd is sprouting umbrellas. Some people gather their jackets over their heads. It's enormously comforting to see this transformation, this mobilization effort in response to the anticipated.

Soon the rain is falling in generous drops. I walk away as far as possible from the sound of the woman's voice, while the wind picks up and the rain starts to spit slantwise. Of course I have no umbrella or raincoat. I didn't even take a look at the weather in the newspaper. My light jacket flaps behind me. I stop under a tree to get my bearings. People stream around me up the hill, some squealing as the rain intensifies, others cowering under their makeshift portable shelters of newspapers or garbage bags. Those who have umbrellas share them. Groups of four and six huddle under the extra plastic that must have been brought for the Quilt. I walk past a man with a videocamera who has taken shelter to film the storm from an open Porta-John. Under some of the trees, the demonstrators for justice carry on as if nothing has changed. I cut across the trailing crowd and head for the Monument. Others have this idea too, all of us already soaked so we've ceased to care how soon we reach cover, but determined to reach it nonetheless. I don't want to have come this far, even by accident, to see nothing. Why not, in a rainstorm, for once in my life, head for the highest ground in the city? Against all sense, yes, but this close to seeing some-

1989

thing, some great movement of people across the vast space of the Mall, I'd be a fool to try to stay safe.

Despite the pounding rain, the sod beneath my feet is reassuring and firm, clover and Bermuda grass matted down from many human steps before mine. I run with the others to the stone needle at the top of the hill.

If I've gotten another cold or pneumonia again, it's been gotten by now. If I made a mistake coming here, it's made. What matters is that I'm one among a dozen who witness now a fluke of time and direction precise and fantastic: the rain stops for us only, in an enchanted circle of maybe thirty feet, as suddenly as though we'd ducked through a door no one else can see.

The Monument blocks the rain because the wind cuts in almost horizontally, due east. It's as if a knife blade could save a clan of ants. Two park rangers guard its meager entrance, but no one is trying to get in. We have all we need out here. We watch the crowd boil over the great lawn below.

It isn't quiet up on this hill. The wind is now whipping umbrellas inside out and swiping hats. People are chattering and leaning against one another, weak with laughter, fatigue, and relief. The rangers chant, "*Please* get *off* the *hill*. Everybody get *off* the *hill*." They're afraid lightning will strike the high ground and we will hold the federal government responsible. One by one, two by two, the others leave the hill as instructed. I can't believe it's so easy for them to go. These are the same people, I am sure, who won't budge an inch when they're standing in the aisle of the bus at rush hour and the driver repeatedly urges them to move back. I shout to be heard over the wind and the bellowing guards: "Who's afraid of a little rain? We're already wet, what more can happen? What more can happen?"

Most of them ignore me. One or two look back and then away with shamed grins. They shrug and smile and carry on down the hill as instructed. Most will forget immediately their strange luck, to be in the only spot on the Mall where the rain couldn't penetrate. Only a handful will go home to recount the story to a loved one, saying, *Can you believe it?* and *Wish you'd been with me*. So few, so very few will turn to

45

1989

one another years from now and say, *Remember the day the rain stopped, just for us?* I'll be long gone.

So I'm alone. The guards' dark glasses drill into my cold back. I take a step down, then another, slowly like I used to do when I played tag as a kid, teasing whoever was It, acting like I'd be such an easy catch, just a hand's breadth away, such a sitting duck, then—

"Ha!" I pull into a low crouch and spring into the air to land as far down the hill as I can. I hit and skid, mud jetting under my sneakers as I slide against the unforgiving ground. There I lie inhaling the cold draft of rain and listening to the fifty flags whipping at their poles around the Monument. This is where I am, for the time that I am.

In the cab home, I notice I don't have my watch. Just as well. I would have ruined it in the rain. It's hard to tell where the sun is behind the clouds. It's probably three o'clock or so. My wet clothes are heavy, and I'm thinking of a bath and a long sleep.

Rich is bent over in our garden, pulling weeds out one small clump at a time. He straightens up when he sees me and swipes at his brow with an ungloved hand, leaving a muddy streak.

"What happened?"

"I went walking in a well. How's the garden?"

"Never mind that. Let's get you inside. God you're impossible, honey."

"You have to pay the driver. I'm out of cash." I fall into his arms. "I'm wiped," I complain.

He holds me carefully in a temporary, incomplete circle. I smell the earth and wet herb on his skin. His hands on me are chilly damp but his breath is warm. He takes me inside and leaves me in the bathroom to pull off my sneakers and wet socks. After he has paid the driver he comes back and peels down my jeans for me, has me stand and raise my hands so he can pull away my heavy sweatshirt. For a moment as I hug my icy arms I have no quarrel with my body. It's performing as I need it to, warming up steadily, no matter what new miseries might be gestating in its layers.

Rich pulls back the covers of our bed and lays me down. He takes off his own clothes and ducks under the blankets too.

I turn from him, pressing my back against his belly, and we drift

1989

together toward sleep. I rub my feet together to savor the ache of my long walk. His hand is draped over my hip, sometimes brushing my stomach, sometimes not, radiating the warmth of the deeply familiar. One darker freckle on his callused index finger seems to hover, bedded in his skin. Like an eye that seems to float free but in fact is only suspended, connected to a structure, a context, a root. Or like a kite tethered to the earth by a string but still able to climb and climb. There are limits everywhere. Also connections, buried or invisible, I mean to everything. What we look at can travel, but the eye itself can only roll and flicker in its socket. The eye can see everything but itself. If you look at the sun it's all over. Before I can form the next thought, I fall . . .

※

Rain gives way to an early snow just before Thanksgiving. Bed rest again, for my second long cold of the season. I pray for inches of snow, enough so the world will stop, not just my life. Listlessly I page through the newspaper, putting off the work I've had sent from the office. Alice is pitching in on Courtland Arms until I feel better. Schaeffer, our recently installed wonderboy, is using my desk this week until we can clear out the library for his permanent office. I keep drawing up ambitious plans for the house, most of which I know won't fly. There are medical bills now, and if I look directly at myself in the mirror I know I don't look well. Each morning I rouse myself long enough to see Rich off to work, and then I burrow back into bed with sketch pad and pencils. I haven't drawn exclusively by hand since I was an intern. Sometimes I sit at Rich's desk to draw. My own study has always been just a corner of whatever room I care to set it up in at the time, although that could change if the dreams from my drawings came true. The snow stops by midmorning, velvet on the trees and buildings. Whether it melts or freezes by tomorrow, I will still be here. That's what I know.

※

"Why don't you sit up a little straighter for me, David? Breathe in. Good. Again. Good. Okay, watch yourself for another week, get a lot of rest and liquids, and after that if you feel okay you can cut the Bactrim

1989

back to three times a week. You know that's a permanent part of your regimen now, right?"

Lerner holds my chin in his hand, jaw gaping slightly in sympathy while he examines the white muck on my tongue. "This isn't clearing up. How long did you say you'd had this?"

I shrug and tug my sleeve down where the nurse took blood.

"How is the AZT this time? Okay? If it doesn't work for you, there are other things we can use, a whole new class of drugs they're looking at now. You could be a candidate for a trial." He hands me two new prescriptions and the familiar pamphlets. "All things considered, you are doing fine. You really are. You are doing a fine job taking care of yourself. You both are."

Rich smiles the pleased smile of a good steward. In the waiting room as we leave he is still smiling, shepherding me along with a hand on my arm that squeezes just a shade too tight, fingers that whiten a little with the nerves and the pressure. I smile too, reassuring him, knowing I am at the moment his whole life, his cause and his project, as the house we share is becoming my project. He smiles, I smile, we both smile—brave, big, pep-squad smiles—at the only remaining patient of the day, a stranger we haven't seen before, maybe new to this as I no longer am. He is here by himself, reading a magazine with apparent absorption. Rich ushers me out, through the hospital's great glass doors, past the water pond and koi and bronze plaque declaring that all this beauty is in the memory of someone's beloved dead.

1990

This past winter seemed as if it always started with the same morning, dawn, streets silent, even the birds still asleep, and the blinds throwing blue shadows across our bed. There I was, home so many days, sketch pad at hand, waiting for better light. A single bird would begin its seesaw singing, and another would answer meep-meep-meep. The traffic picked up, heavy engines of buses and trucks on their regular routes, the jangling of dog leashes and shouts of the trash men and construction workers.

On days when I ventured out to the office, I kept passing faces I thought I remembered, not the faces of people I knew so well, but of people familiar from the clubs and haunts I used to frequent before I met Rich. It's amazing how old we've gotten in just these few years. Two in a row I saw in a week. One was a waiter who used to be at Paolo's when it was still a good place to go, and then at Mr. Smith's on the Hill. He had black hair back then, so dark it was blue, a gelled and deliberate mess that fell over his high fine forehead in coils. When I saw him his head seemed rounder with its fringe of silver ringing a shining pate. He carried a briefcase. Then at the bus stop one day I saw a guy Henry used to go out with, after Gary. His Cupid plumpness had slid off his bones toward his center, where he carried a medium-sized paunch he had to reach beneath to dig into his pockets for coins.

Now it's spring. The beggars, mental cases, and outcasts seem to blossom under the greening trees — they are always here, of course, all winter, but they become more visible now, maybe because life outside is easier. Or maybe we see more of them because we are outside more. Ragged Elijahs with belongings in trash bags and grocery carts at street corners or emerging from alleys or sitting mute and dead-eyed on the retaining wall outside a posh condo building, or chattering and ecstatic

1990

amid the office workers who picnic in McPherson Square. I remember more than one of these walking agonies from many years and harsh winters ago, people persisting into a new decade despite the obvious odds: the black man in a gray rain poncho whose deep basso voice could crack rocks or soothe an infant to sleep; the puckish young guy with a muscle disorder who spastically "dances" to Marvin Gaye tunes that play from the boom box strapped to his wheelchair. Or the woman on a perpetual campaign to avenge her dead son and many others subsumed by mushrooming conspiracies, the intricacies of which she's taken elaborate pains to convey on a series of cardboard signs she ties to herself and tapes to the paneled van she apparently lives in. There's another, a calm woman with a scarf tied on her head, her face placid and friendly except for the walleye that seems ready to spring from its socket.

It wouldn't surprise me to look out our back window some morning and see that woman, or several like her, taking refuge in our leaky new addition. The broken back wall of our house almost seems to invite such encroachment. This weekend the crew was supposed to finish framing in the sunroom, but the rain stopped their work. The scent of mud and wet lumber settled over the house along with an eerie stillness. We are alone for the first time in a month. While we share the newspaper and morning coffee, a starling slips through the plastic over the hole we punched for the skylight, battering itself against the unfinished walls until it lies twitching on the concrete subfloor. I scoop the bird up with my bare hand to throw it back outside.

"David!" Rich holds up a section of the newspaper. "Use this, for God's sake. That thing is full of parasites."

Can't I take an ordinary risk? The bird refuses to fly free. Even after I throw it into the yard, it comes back, confused. This time, at Rich's insistence, I put on yellow dishwashing gloves to retrieve it. I throw it outside and it lands beneath the neighbors' maple. A few minutes later I find the bird in the grass, breast heaving, bright eyes rolling excitedly at the sky.

"It was the gloves," I insist to Rich. "See, I injured it."

Rich silently fetches a shovel and brings its metal pan down on the bird without flinching, then digs a small grave.

We've had permitting problems, hassles getting materials on time, a

1990

carpenter who skipped out when he got a better job. Now this dead bird in our backyard. But we have broken open the back of the house, so there's no stopping now. The back yard is excavated, and we've laid a slab for the new room. Yesterday when I came home I found workmen standing around solemnly in our trashed back yard, with my contractor Carl off to one side shaking his head.

"We got a little problem, Dave," he told me.

"What kind?"

"Hit a main. Just nicked it without meaning to."

"You're kidding." Through the gaping hole where our back wall had been, I watched the front door open and Rich come walking back. "What's all this?"

"We probably have to excavate the back yard."

Rich looked around, blinked, sighed, and said, "Why don't we order in for dinner?"

At bedtime I found him plucking through the stack of papers on my desk, pinching sheets between thumb and forefingers and pulling on his glasses.

"We should discuss whether to do this," he said. "How do you know this contractor isn't taking us for a ride?"

"This isn't optional, Rich. You saw all the water."

"You know, every time you decide to do something without discussion, you give me this line about how indisputable it is." Rich grabbed another estimate in the pile. "Like the lead thing. People have been living with lead in their houses for decades. If you leave it alone it won't do you any harm. Why not just forget taking out walls?"

I worked to keep any note of contempt out of my voice. "There are walls we need to take out. And since lead is unsafe once it's airborne—"

"Yes, yes, I'm not stupid. It's moot now, anyway. You got your way. But this other thing, I mean it sounds to me like they ought to do it free if they hit a pipe."

"Carl's already given me a deal."

"So he says."

"Well, a problem won't go away just because we want it to," I insisted. "The point is, when you do this kind of work you've got to expect some things to go wrong."

53

1990

"You do?"

"Yes. And when something is wrong, you correct it and move on."

"When you can."

"That's right. When you can."

"Well, at what point do you admit that you can't, David? How far do you go, how much do you drain your bank account and try your patience before you say enough?"

"Why do we keep having this conversation? And why do you keep asking me as if I know the answer? You're the one who started this, not me, Rich, remember? And if you're freaking out now, I am very worried. Because we're not nearly through."

He knows it, too. He knows we'll have to dig out the yard. He hasn't said a word about it tonight. He just needed to lodge that token protest, to go through the motions of control. I brought a couple of bottles of wine and his favorite movie home tonight. We settle down to watch *The Lavender Hill Mob*. Alec Guinness and his partner spiral madly down the Eiffel Tower, chasing after school girls who've been sold gold souvenir replicas, encased in lead, by mistake. We'd seen the movie before, and I remembered this scene, but not the fact that they are laughing, the two men. Running down the stairs, tearing after gold they've lost, gold worth millions, gold trapped in six little copies of the Eiffel Tower, these two men facing prison and chasing after their last-ditch chance, are laughing.

※

Soon the garden Rich has built up over years in our tiny yard, terraced with railroad ties, will be trampled mud. I offer to help him move plants, but he says he'd rather do it himself. He's already exposed the bare ground in most places, transplanting his favorites to the front yard or to containers that will live in our new sunroom eventually. Now he's ripping out the Carolina jessamine and the vinca and sweet flag in clumped handfuls, composted all but a few hardy cuttings that he's nursing in an improvised holding bed out front. So the ground is already churned up now, clods of earth on the sidewalk. "Maybe we'll wind up saving on the excavation," I joke, but he doesn't laugh. He stands back to see what kind of space he will have left once the sun-

1990

room's in place. "It's going to be a little pocket courtyard like the ones in Amsterdam," he says. "Very crowded and colorful."

He can't be resenting my design for the sunroom already, can he? Taking just a few feet of this miserly yard? It wouldn't be the first time I have watched him cheerily make the most of a choice he feels is foisted on him, all the while fuming, waiting for the moment when he can tick off ways in which he's been so good, such a sport about whatever injury's been done his intentions. Yet he's so proud of his work as an economist, the fundamental fact of which is that no one does anything without perceived benefit. So what's the benefit of martyrdom for him? It's not only with me: His relationships with family are basically nothing but the Good Sport game. I'll tell you what the benefit is. It's money in the bank for him. He'll hoist the hollies and oleanders into big oak half-barrels, rip out his garden's ground cover and fuss over the cuttings he's preparing for friends who've asked. Then he'll save the resentment until the right moment arrives when he can throw back in my face what a caring, selfless partner he is. The first time I set him off without meaning to, back it will all come: the goodwill, the care, the cheerfulness, my God, the consideration and patience and will to make things work between us. It feels good, I think. I think he enjoys the suspense. Maybe I have begun to, too.

The phone rings. It's my dad.

"Son? How are you doing?"

"Oh, fine. Fine. Rich and I were just out in the garden." Behind me I hear a crash and a curse.

"Listen, I know this is short notice, but I'm planning a visit up there. I'd like to stay with you if that's all right."

"Oh?" My dad hasn't once visited me since I moved here. What has Jodie told him? "Sure, okay, I guess."

"I can stay in a hotel. I mean with the house being worked on and all."

"Well. The back is kind of a mess, but our upstairs is still okay. No, come on up."

Rich calls me from out back. "Be there in a sec, Rich. Dad, I need to go. Can we talk later today?"

"Sure, sure. How about I come in two weeks?"

1990

"So soon? I mean, okay."

Rich has tipped over our blue bird fountain, the one we bought at a tag sale in Cape Cod. He's scraping the pieces out of the dirt when I come back out. "First you kill a bird," he says, "then I destroy our bird fountain. What does this tell us?"

"I didn't kill the bird. It died because of your fastidious nature."

"It died because I care so deeply about you."

"Right. Okay. Let's test that deep caring, then: That was my dad. He's coming up to visit."

"Oh. Just when I was thinking things couldn't get worse."

"What?"

"Just a joke, David. You just joked about it yourself."

"It's my dad. I can joke about my dad."

He sits back and looks up at me a moment, then returns to his work. He grasps a clump of vines from the bottom and yanks their roots out, tugging and then reeling the foliage in with a pop like pulling at zippers. He throws them to the compost.

We go to bed exhausted, sick of working on the house, sick of each other, sick of the arguments. I dream I am tapping on the walls we plan to demolish, listening for the tenor note of plaster, the baritone of drywall. I put my hands through without expecting to, grasping the surface and pulling it away in gummy fistfuls, and when I turn I find the floor rising into steps I wasn't looking for. Rooms from my parents' house have grafted themselves to the upstairs hallway. I open the door to our bedroom and find my sister, Jodie, playing with a piñata with neighbor kids who've long since grown up and gone away.

As a kid I would wake up like this after a dream and lay hardly breathing, waiting until I heard my father prowl the house, checking each lock and window in turn to make sure we were safe. He cracked the door of my room and put his head in. With my eyes closed, I felt his presence there, and though night after night I tried to will him to come closer, stand over me, and put his hand across my forehead as my mother would have done, night after night he just walked up the hall and went back to bed.

1990

I was always begging my parents to take me to see the new shopping malls, new buildings, and once a brand new airport. It wasn't the projects themselves I was after, but their models: Pressing my face against the glass display box, I'd stare at the tiny silver pools, the doll figures and trees, the miniature cars in the parking lot. I would walk hand in hand with my parents through places I'd just seen in miniature, stopping when I recognized a fountain, an entrance, or other landmark. My father had a joke when I did this. "You are here," he'd say.

One birthday my parents bought me the Game of Life, with its plastic car pieces, raised mountain ridges, green countryside, and brown towns. I played it a few times, but more often I set it up and added to it, little trees made from toothpicks and painted newspaper, pocket mirrors for ponds, and a modern office building made of stacked velvet jewel boxes that once held my mother's earrings. After my cousins lost most of the gamepieces over several Thanksgivings, Jodie and I still sometimes spread the board out on the floor, spinning the wheel and watching it land on all the choices we couldn't play anymore.

It was years before I understood that the men designing life-size versions of those crisp complexes were not like kings, decreeing where the streets and people would go, but more like the Biblical prophets and storybook magicians whose successes rely on the pleasure of insecure royalty. Still I wanted to build things. At first I had a fuzzy notion how to make buildings, and I saw the similarity between the shapes they taught in school and the structures around me. From the Astrodome in Houston, the first monumental new building I had actually visited, I learned to draw triangles that united into curves. I wanted to build something like it, transform the rules of shapes at a scale that everyone could see, so strangers who'd never met would at least have in common this place I'd made.

I drew and redrew the domed monkey bars at school, counting the twenty red triangles that pressed points and bases into the grass intermittently. I looked up through the center to memorize the ten white metal rods framing the sky in triangles, welded by their noses into now a pentagon, now a star. I had better teachers later, but I was never a better student for drafting than I was that spring.

I was fascinated by the table of circular measure in the back of my composition book, beside the compass of angles and the other tables of measure: linear, surface, liquid, dry, and time. Someone had even calculated, and reported, the weight of air: thirteen-and-a-half cubic feet to the pound. But it was the circular table, transforming the familiar rules of time into rules for space, that caught me up on long afternoons when I was supposed to be doing my homework for history, or science, or math. I was indulging in a kind of math, not of solutions but of philosophy. It was as satisfying as making a dome from triangles without bending their sides, to consider that sixty seconds equaled a minute of the earth's surface, and that the minute had a value in distance—69.16 miles at the equator. It reminded me of the way my father had taught me to tell time by putting twelve pennies in a circle on the kitchen table after dinner, patiently explaining how the short soda straw was the hour and the long one the minute. Afterward he'd let me keep the pennies whether I did well or not. I put them in my mouth to warm them, pulled them out and tossed them in the air till they were cold, then put them in my mouth again, tasting the blood tang of copper.

I built a Styrofoam model of the planets and sun in my room for the science fair, in secret, and plotted out a scale for the distances. I hid the solar system in my closet while I made improvements, rigging fishing line and clothes hangers so that when the tiny blue planet swung around the sun, it dragged the black shell of the universe along in its wake. I wouldn't let my mom and dad see anything until the judging.

The day we took turns at the microphone in the auditorium, my dad was working. That year he taught driving for a private company, and he seemed always to have lessons when I wanted him around. Though he said he'd try to make it, I knew he would never show up. My mother was there late, leaning on a column at the back, nodding and holding up her hands every time I looked out over the crowd. Other mothers smiled at their children too, but when Mom did she nodded so much that her hair shook and her purse jangled its contents. Her red mouth traced dangerous circles: *lOve yOu. dOing gOOd.*

prOud OfyOu. I thought if she spoke to me or tried to touch me afterward, I would do my best to ignore her.

"Thousands of years ago," I began, my voice shaking, "Eratosthenes of Alexandria measured the earth." I was too short for the mike. When I tried to adjust it, I sent out deafening feedback. "With just a wooden stick, Eratosthenes used shadows from the sun to estimate the earth's circumference. He calculated it as fifty times the distance between Alexandria and Aswan, twenty-five thousand miles altogether, within one hundred miles of the right answer."

No one but my mother was paying much attention. The other students scuffled and giggled as they waited their turn or ignored me. Our science teacher stood below the stage's apron, scowling out until the room was quiet again. I told whoever would listen about al-Kashi of Samarkand, how he invented the table of circular measure by calculating *pi* to sixteen places. Later, explorers had to rediscover what he already knew: The universe is curved just like the earth.

I won Honorable Mention, after the incubator that hatched live chicks, the heat reaction with steel wool, and the life cycle of tomatoes. Mom helped me load my universe into the car and took me to Baskin Robbins. At home, I set the whole thing up again in the front hallway, with the purple ribbon so I could show my dad as soon as he got home. He came in by the back door when dinner was already crusty in the oven. I dragged him to the front room.

"Nice work, Dave," he said, loosening his collar and hunting in his pocket until he came up with a handkerchief. "Glad to finally get a look." He blew his nose loudly and turned to go.

"Dad." My voice, making him turn and wait, drew something tight and heavy between us. "Don't you notice anything?"

He sighed and wiped his hand down his face from top to bottom, as if to remove the day's work from it. "Son, I just got home, I haven't even taken a piss yet, and I'm not in the mood for games. What is it you want me to see? Just tell me."

I opened my mouth and nothing came out. I was scared I'd cry or worse, that I might yell at him, and then get shouted into silence, and then probably cry anyway and no stopping it then.

1990

"Come on, okay, I'm looking, I'm looking. What am I going to do with you? What are you so upset about?"

I couldn't look at the model or him, so I focused on the worn yellow carpet in the front hall. The point was not that I'd almost won. I already knew that wasn't good enough. It's just that I couldn't have made the model without remembering the clock and how my Dad had taught me to tell time. I wanted him to see what I saw now, that a clock was a little universe, or the universe a big clock. For either one to make sense, you needed to know what was connected, what it pulled, and how far you had to go before you were back at the beginning.

※

Two weeks later, I am laid up again. Rich goes instead of me to pick my father up. They've never met and there was no time for me to call Dad and tell him it wouldn't be me. I hope it's going well. At least I talked Dad into the extra sixty dollars for the round trip to fly into National Airport, so even if the drive is uncomfortably awkward, it won't be long.

I don't hear the two of them come in the front door, because I am sitting in a lawn chair out back in two mufflers and Rich's wool Dodgers jacket, watching the workmen like a hawk.

"Buster!" says my Dad. I turn stiffly—my neck is bothering me too, in the raw March wind—to see him just the same as ever, almost stepped out of time, back into my life. He doesn't look older this time as he usually does. I'm the one, now. "Rich told me you're sick, what are you doing out here?"

"I am sick, Dad," I say, without budging. "Don't get too close."

"Son, come in. You'll catch your death out here."

But he's wrong about that. I think that it's inside, cozy in bed, flipping through magazines and waiting to feel better, where I'd catch my death.

"I'm okay. I get my rest."

"He does, Mr. Baum," says Rich. "He takes excellent care of himself." That exchange tells me everything. Dad knows, probably from Jodie.

It's clear that he and Rich talked about it in the car on the way back. I should have gone; I should have dressed and gone with him.

Never mind. Dad, always good at being distracted from the heart of things, now inspects the sunken pit where our porch was with the speculative passion of a high school physics whiz, the ground-up soil and rocks all around, the bags of Quik-Crete and sheets of drywall. "Wow. You fellas took the back off the house."

But Rich is still on the job. "He naps every day, and I make sure of it. If I'm at work, I call after lunch just to check in."

"Well, you look good, son. Really, you look good."

"Anyway, let's all go in. Stop, I'm fine, I'm fine." Dad keeps his hand outstretched anyway. The veins stand out on the back of this hand, blue and swollen and crooked as old rivers on the terrain of loose skin and fine bones. In the hot kitchen I pull off my mufflers but leave the jacket on. Dad says, "Smells terrific in here."

"I made a stew," says Rich. "It's vegetarian."

My Dad laughs. "Better than a poke in the eye with a sharp stick." It's something he has said since I was a kid, one of those repetitive phrases parents specialize in. "If I have time to wash up, though—"

"Right this way," says Rich. The two of them smile warmly like old friends. "I'll set you up in our study. Come on."

※

I take the steps to my office slowly, keeping my eyes down so I don't slip. My legs feel hollowed out and close to collapse. Alice is in our office already, sitting in my chair, enjoying the view out my window.

"I didn't think you'd be in today." She lifts her coffee cup from where it has ringed the wood on my desk. "The view is so nice from here. I sat here on Friday. I hope you don't mind."

I watch her dribble coffee down her arm. She takes the tissue I hand her, but won't meet my eyes.

"So," she says, "I'm supposed to cover this meeting at the Arlington Planning Department."

"Cover it? You mean go in my place?"

"Meg said she couldn't get a hold of you on Friday."

1990

"I wasn't home, but I left her a return message."

"She must not have gotten it. Anyway, now that you're here, no biggie. We'll just talk to Meg."

"I told her I would be here. That's what I said on her voice mail on Friday."

"I don't have to go."

"No, no. It's okay. That's not my point. What's this?" The color rendering up on her screen looks like what I was sketching out by hand last week for the Arlington project.

"Oh. I just came in over the weekend to flesh out some of your concepts. You can present them; I mean they are your ideas. I was going to give you credit."

"Alice, calm down. You can cover the meeting if Meg asked you to. I have a lot to do here."

"You sure?"

"Sure. Just— Bill Hagen knows I am still the architect?"

"Of course."

"I don't know what might have gotten around by this time. Know what I mean?"

"Not exactly." She is shutting down the rendering and clearing the screen, so casually that I know she knows.

"Just tell them I still work here, okay? Full time."

She finally turns to look at me, but only for a moment before she drops her eyes. "I'm sorry, David."

"About what?"

"I don't know. Sitting at your desk, I guess. Doing some of your work."

Anxiety has a sweet smell, like a ruined garden or those awful lilies they sell cheaply on the street, the ones with pollen that crusts your shirtfront and nose. I smelled it last at my mother's funeral, that waxy cloy, mixed after the service with the fragrance of coffee and the scent of warm pot pies and briskets the women brought for my father to freeze. I smelled it on Gary. It's why I steered clear of him toward the end. I thought it was only his illness, but now I think it was all of us around him too. I smell it on Alice.

"You probably ought to talk to Meg," she says. "Just touch base."

1990

My desk has been rearranged slightly, the things I was working on pushed carefully to one side. Someone has even claimed the wall above my computer, and a note is impaled there: "Caution: Sick Mac!"

Alice follows my eyes and reaches over to snap the note down and toss it away. "That's been taken care of."

"What happened?"

"I found a virus on my PC at home after working here, and I don't know which one got it first. We had a guy out to run disk scans or something, and you're all fixed up. Apparently there are only so many viruses. They're very simple when you get it down to the basic level."

"The wonders of modern technology."

"Amazing, isn't it?" She packs up her portfolio. "Don't want to be late for that meeting."

"Right."

When she's gone I open all the programs on my computer in sequence without a disk in the slot. But it's no use, I don't really know what I am looking for. Then I notice Meg leaning in my doorway. "David. You're in today."

"I never said I wouldn't be."

"Alice's covering the Arlington County meeting."

"Yes, I know. Did you get my message? I did say I would be in today, and I had things to show them."

"I got that message this morning. When were you planning to show this work to me before representing my firm to a client?"

"It's a shirtsleeves meeting, Meg. They are working sketches."

"Not now they aren't. Alice and I went over them this weekend, and she turned out some first-rate work around your concepts. Which I have every faith you could have done, had you been here."

"Okay, Meg. Why don't we get out of the office later, like we used to do, and talk?"

She's going to take me off the project, I can feel it. Maybe she will fire me outright. Do longevity and loyalty count at all? If I played the health card, would she keep me on out of pity or shuttle me out all the faster?

Alice comes back after lunch, buzzing about how much Bill loved the ideas. Not "mine" or "yours," only the cautious neuter. For the rest of the afternoon I stare out the window more or less the whole time, pretending to work when I have to but otherwise letting myself be distracted by the kids in the playground below. At five the playground is taken over by a string of couriers who've piled their bikes up as if they're about to torch them. That huddle of metal is a gesture of self-help, I know: the messengers gathering the tools of their livelihood so no one can make off with them. They're playing hackie in a circle, bumping the small sand bag from player to player with their feet and heads.

At five-fifteen I clear my desk off, line up my pencils for tomorrow or whenever I'm in again, put my desk watch back in the drawer, and fold my hands. I should go up to Meg's office, but I can't. Whatever is wrong, I don't want to know. I want to cancel and stay in the dark. When I make myself take the steps up to Meg's level, I find she is hanging in her doorway too, waiting to get it over with. Maybe Meg would also like to go home.

"Ready?"

"Yeah, ready." I motion for her to go ahead of me.

※

"So the Courtland Arms project is still stalled in court," she begins. This is old news, but I humor her along. Both of us know we're here to talk about something else. I can't tell who is supposed to start.

"I'm told the tenants' association doesn't have the pull to put the developer out of business, even if they win a settlement," I say.

"Bunch of old biddies," Meg leans over to take a light from me. "I suppose they want us to just wait for each of them to die."

"Meg, you're all heart."

"Don't you want to start the project?"

"Sure, but we knew this would happen." It could be two years or more before the project is realized. I want to have that long, at least. Meg put me on the project because I could stand the long haul. She must know I might not be able to now.

When we came in, the bar was still nearly empty. Now almost every table is full of office workers, women with their shoes off under the table, men with their ties loosened. Meg sips from her beer while the

1990

head is still high, setting it back down in the nest of wet napkins on the tabletop. The faded newspaper clippings under the glass tell lurid stories from the early years of the century, detailing the aftermaths of heavy drinking and domestic disputes. Meg takes another cigarette from the pack. When she pulls back her lips, her fake left incisor flashes bright white against her real teeth. I wag my match out, inhaling. The tobacco is at the perfect, musky point before going stale.

"David, I'm just going to jump in. I'm concerned about how much you've been out of the office lately. I worry that your plate is too full."

"I'm not sure what you mean."

"Well, the amount of work you are doing versus what you have done for us in the past . . . I mean, to be blunt, you're getting sick, right? And it's long term."

What an optimistic phrase: *long term.*

"You don't even have to answer. I'm not an idiot. I know what's going on. Just— Why haven't you told me so we could work this out?"

"Would you, in my shoes?"

"I don't think I would lie to my employer."

For as long as I have known Meg I have never seen her soften for more than a second. "I didn't lie. I didn't know when to tell you."

"I could tell you when to tell me. When I make you the project architect on a major job. When I am obviously grooming you for partnership, that's when."

"Would you really? Would that be the time you'd tell your boss you're sick?"

"David, keep your voice down. If you'd included us earlier, if you'd let us help make a Plan B—"

"I'm going to take care of that. I was planning to take Alice out on visits with me."

"Excuse me if this is indelicate, but what happens down the line? We'd like to be supportive, but frankly we're too small to have much leeway."

"Do you want me to resign?"

I can see the relief flicker in her eyes. She would love it. She picks up her empty glass for a sip, then puts it down. She murmurs some reassuring platitude about loyalty and family, and signals the waiter impa-

1990

tiently. He brings both of us fresh beers, although I didn't order one. I watch Meg pour hers straight up instead of tilting the glass. The foam cascades over the lip of the glass, coats the sides, and pools on the table.

"Dammit. Sorry." She takes my napkin without asking and dabs at the front of her suit. "I want to propose a different arrangement, David. Suppose you took a day or two off each week. They could be floating days for now, so it's pretty much like what you're doing, only it's official and you're not taking sick days."

"But I'm taking less money?"

"But you have your insurance. And you share your work with the other associates so that, God forbid, if something should happen and you're out for an extended period of time . . ."

Like for good.

". . . they could step in and spell you for as long as it takes you to get back on your feet."

"So you're offering me more flexibility, in exchange for a cut in pay."

"And partnering more closely with Alice."

I shouldn't make a fuss. What she is offering is practical. Of course, she could have decided to let things go on as they are, not "offered" me a pay cut, but there it is. Public acknowledgment that I'm not worth what I was. Why not let the old ladies die in place? What's wrong with getting some slack for a year or two when everyone around you has decades to burn?

"David, have you known for very long?"

I twist a cocktail straw around my finger. The waiter pours off the rest of Meg's beer and takes the empty bottle.

"You don't have to give me an answer right away, about this new arrangement," she says. "Think about it, let me know, say, Friday. You know I value you, David. We've got time to work this out."

Maybe you do, maybe I don't. I can already hear Henry insisting this is discrimination, telling me to fight, take it all the way to court if I have to. But I know as well as Meg this tired feeling in my bones will come on me more and more often, and when it does, it's her disability insurance that will support me. It would be a relief not to call in sick so constantly, to have an arrangement above board. Flexible time and no guilt.

"I think this will give us both what we need." She snaps her gold

1990

card down on the table, another task checked off her list. She'd like to feel good about how all this works out. She'd like to be able to live with herself afterward.

※

Rich has outdone himself tonight. After determining that Dad is indeed a meat eater and long since abandoned any pretense of keeping kosher, it's as if Rich transformed himself into the chef to Ernest Hemingway. One night we eat broiled buffalo burgers, another night game fowl, and tonight we're having venison. No kidding. I cower before my slab of game at one end of the table while Rich lights the candles and invites us to tuck in with a flourish I've never seen him use before.

"Well, I must say, we are eating well around here," says Dad.

"Yes, and we only had to meet that once with the World Wildlife Fund's lawyers."

"Very funny, David. Have some mustard sauce."

I'm not hungry. The light in here is dim enough but everything seems to swim in front of my eyes with an unhealthy brightness. I squint and try to cut my meat.

"Everything all right, honey?"

I nod, and just that little movement throws me so completely I think I'll have to leave the table. Gripping my chair, I steady myself and wait, counting silently. One, two . . .

"So what's doing at work today, son? Big project? You were so late to get home."

"It wasn't such a good day. I'm not going in enough, you know. So push is coming to shove on a couple of projects." Three, four, five . . .

"Well, the work at home here is bound to be a distraction. And me staying underfoot."

"Oh, no, David and I have so enjoyed having you. Anyway, they'll be sealing up the back wall before we know it. Then maybe we should take a bit of a break from renovating."

"The rest isn't going to be so bad; it's mostly decorative work." Six, seven . . .

"David. You look a little green."

"Excuse me."

1990

I push back from the table and make it down the hall just in time, crouching over the toilet in the brash bathroom light, insisting through the door that I am fine, pulling myself up to the counter when I am finished, rinsing my mouth and swallowing a thick worm of toothpaste before finally opening the door.

Dad leans in first. Rich pushes past him to hold me up.

"You know, I'm pretty sick. I think I may need to go to the emergency room."

"Is it food poisoning?"

"I don't think it could be. I've been feeling so bad for so long."

Dad clenches his fists, balls them into his armpits. "Do you want a cold rag? Water?" My mom would know just what to do.

Rich throws some things into an overnight bag and drives both of us to the emergency room. It's not too full, luckily, just a kitchen worker with his hand in a bloody dishtowel, an old woman with enormous blue-veined legs, and a college kid with a skateboard and a swelling knot over one eye. My father sits near the exit as Rich has me admitted, one hand jammed into his hip pocket, jingling his keys.

After I am deemed financially fit to treat, they shuttle me off to a bright examining room to give my history five times, along with urine, blood, and a stool sample. None of this is meant to make me feel better. When I ask for a painkiller for my head they tell me to hang on just a few more minutes, because they want me to talk with the doctor and describe what the pain is like. As if a Tylenol 4 could make me forget.

Rich stays with me the whole time. Sometimes my father puts his anxious face to the window of the examining room, and sometimes he comes in to stand against the wall, not quite ready to look me in the eye. One time when we are alone he smooths back my hair and asks, "How could this be happening to my boy?" I don't know who he is talking to, and he makes it sound like I am dying. I shrug away nervously. Finally a doctor arrives.

"Well, this could be one of several types of meningitis. That's the most likely scenario. Have you been having trouble breathing? No? We're going to culture for pneumonia. But you had a lot of vomiting, so this may be a new flu. The other possibility is a drug or food reaction. How long have you been on AZT?"

"Just a few months."

"Mmm. Of course, the real fun begins if this is a combination of several things. Say, what's your CD4 count?"

He asks like he wants to know my bowling average. I feel like recommending he check with the five residents who've already collected this information from me, presumably for his benefit. "About 200."

"When did you find out you were positive?"

I glance at my father.

"About four years ago."

Dad makes a sound like he's had a very slender blade slid gently into his throat-hollow. Rich pats his arm. The doctor makes a little sound too, as he scribbles something on my chart: a long low whistle. "We'd like to check you in overnight, see how you do, and schedule you for more tests. Have you had an MRI, a brain scan, for cytomegalovirus?"

"I've had a blood test. It was positive."

"Okay. That might be acting up. I'd like to run a brain scan."

"If it seems necessary."

"It does. MRI." He writes it down, my blessing on the procedure clearly a formality. "What about lumbar puncture?" he asks.

"A what?"

"We'll order one." He writes it. "How is your head?"

"I really, really want a painkiller. I've asked several times."

"Feel like you might throw up again?"

"Not at the moment."

"Okay." He writes that down.

Finally, my painkiller comes. It's an oral dose first, to tide me over, which is good, because they have trouble finding a decent vein for the IV. The nurse grabs and grabs at my hand, thumping sometimes and sometimes sticking a needle in. I feel it all but hardly care. They park me, with my street clothes in my lap, in a wheelchair for the trip up to my room. My father's face looms in as he tells me he's going to take a cab back home. I ask what time it is, and I hear someone answer, but then forget. More than midnight. The hospital feels secret and

1990

peaceful, owned by the night shift nurses, who pad along on their white soles, putting their heads in doors to make sure we are all right. Rich pulls a chair right up to the side of my bed. Eventually he sleeps, leaning his cheek against one hand, resting the other hand in its latex glove on the back of mine. When I move, my head starts to thud dully. My hands seem detached from the rest of me anyway, the one near the window floating on top of the stiff sheets, fluids seeping into it from a tube; the other weighted down by Rich. I feel like an unsteady aircraft skimming the air, wobbling in the half dark. Except that would make the ceiling the earth. Every few hours a nurse named Bill comes by to measure and make notes and once in a while to ask me what I need. Rich starts abruptly each time the door glides open, and he echoes Bill, asking me what I want. I don't know where to begin to tell them, so I say nothing, and I thank them. Toward morning I ask for water. A new nurse, Marian, brings me chipped ice.

Before sunrise I am taken downstairs to the MRI room. It's too bright, and in its center is an enormous, hollow white cube with a chrome tray that feeds the patient through. A technician comes in to ease me into position and offer me a few stiff pillows, ear plugs, a black blinder for my eyes. "Some people find these help," he says. He tells me not to move, and he leaves the room. Soon the most awful clatter begins, vibrating every bone in my body and setting every nerve aglow. When the noise shuts off I feel how raw my throat is and I hear this sound, still awful but apparently human. It is me, screaming. That's how calmly I think about it too: oh, it is me and I am screaming.

The attendant comes in again. "Are you uncomfortable?" he asks.

"I'm fucking terrified," I say. Crying, too, I notice. It is me, screaming in this blank room with a stranger, and crying, too. "Where's my dad? Where's Rich?"

"Who?"

"My partner. He's in my room, I want him to come down here."

"What's your room?"

"Dammit. I don't know. It's 3400 North, the . . . I don't know . . . the nervous system unit or something. Don't you have it? Don't you have all the information on me?"

1990

"I'll see what I can do." He goes back into his little room, and I can't move to see whether he's on the phone or not. Anyway, what would that prove? He could be either honoring my request or complaining bitterly to his supervisor about me or talking to his buddy about last night while methodically taking measurements I wouldn't understand of functions I can't see. The air in the room seems to crackle. I hear his voice over the mike into the test room. "Okay, look, let's try one more series, and after that you'll be half done and you can invite anyone you want to come stay in the room with you for the rest of the test."

"What the hell is it, anyway?"

"What is what?"

"What's an MRI, what does it do?"

"Hold still and we'll do this fast."

It's humiliating, to feel desperate like this, to be talked to through a microphone and have your questions shunted aside. To feel how far you are from this guy who sees unlucky stiffs like you every day and goes home without even thinking twice about us. Why should he? Would I give him a second thought if I saw him on the street? What does my life matter to him, or my death either? That's what I feel for the first time, really, in this room: the cold, hollow heart of nonmatter, the state of not mattering a damn.

Afterward I tell the worried-looking couple in the elevator that I am fine. That will become my motto for the next few days. I want to be the pluckiest by-golly AIDS patient they've ever had the pleasure of knowing. I want to charm and warm them, which is pretty pathetic when you think how seldom this has ever been my goal in life. I want to make myself matter to them.

My room is empty except for the equipment and me. Rich has gone home to rest, leaving a note to say he'll be back for lunch. I try to stay sitting up until he comes back, coddling the sickness one way until it catches on and defies me again with a greenish nausea and a rebounding headache so I have to switch to the other position. At five the cafeteria sends up broth, juice, and a cup of Jell-O that I suck straight down like a shot. I feel more alert for a few minutes. I have these windows sometimes, not that the pain ebbs, but it can be viewed from a long way up. I'm having a moment like that when the door opens and in

1990

come Rich and Dad. They stand at the foot of my bed, and Dad solemnly presents a small Mylar balloon with teddy bears on it.

Rich eyes the balloon nervously, hanging on to the metal foot of my bed as if he might float off the ground himself if he doesn't keep his wits about him. "Has the doctor been by?"

"Some guy on rounds was here; he basically just told his students what's wrong with me. Do you mind if I don't talk much?"

It's too bad for them I'm not in intensive care. Those ten-minute limits on visits are a real boon for families. Gary's family couldn't have gotten through the ordeal without them. But these are my lover and my next of kin, game to try anything. I'd like Rich to stay the night again.

I feel so out of it, and sometimes pleasantly so, the moments passing in fits and starts like music, one note to the next, with silences in between that I feel but can't recall. After a few hours I am alone, and there is another liquid meal. I am beginning to be glad of the invention of Jell-O. I savor the strangeness of having my hand appear in front of my face with a spoon in it, although I don't remember lifting it. I ask the nurse for extra ice, and he brings it too late. But he brings me water when I ask, many times all night. Rich comes back. I remember struggling to the bathroom with him beside me, so solid and warm. Then it is morning, and a doctor leans over me in the too-bright light. "How are you feeling?"

"About the same."

"Could you have eaten anything that disagreed with you a few days ago?"

"You mean after all this it could be food poisoning?"

He doesn't answer my question. "You know how doctors diagnose?"

I think he's asking me, but someone else answers. "By process of exclusion."

"How many things do we have to exclude when someone presents with a headache and nausea?"

"Many."

"Many, many, many. Who can tell me what this is likely to be?"

"Meningitis."

"Encephalitis."

"CMV?"

"Some or all of these. Would the MRI tell us conclusively that it's not CMV? Anyone."

"Yes."

"No."

"No. Nothing is conclusive. Course of action?"

"Intravenous antibiotic, then—" something that sounds like "can't cycle here."

"Very good. Mr. Baum, we'd like to start you on an intravenous regimen for CMV as soon as possible."

"For how long?"

"For good. We could install a catheter while you are here and show you how to use it and clean it."

"Like a chest catheter?"

"It is a chest catheter."

Gary had one of those. I never asked what it was for or what it was called. It was toward the end. He lost his sight anyway. Now I know it was CMV, but none of us knew back then. People slipped away in a year, maybe two, while the rest of us pretended nothing was wrong until we had to talk about it. That was not such a long time ago.

"We'd make a small incision in your neck, here, and thread a very small tube under your skin here, to a major artery near your heart. Once a day you'd flush it out, a few times a day you'd inject medicine into it. If you got a new IV medication, in it would go, no problem. In fact, you won't even feel it after a while."

Oh, sure. I'm not ready to have a train station installed above my heart.

"Do I have a choice about this?"

"Always. You can have it put in as outpatient surgery, in a few weeks. I am just suggesting that since I have to give you two medications intravenously while you are here, we would take care of the whole thing quite conveniently."

Conveniently for whom? I shouldn't have uncharitable thoughts about my caregivers. But this man seems so cheerful about installing a permanent orifice in my chest. I will continue to lead a normal life, he says. As if that were anywhere near possible anymore.

73

1990

"Can't you treat me with a regular IV?"

"Do what you're comfortable doing." He's anxious to get on with his rounds, his students are pawing their little notebooks and trying to figure out what lesson this exchange between us holds, now that I won't accept treatment as prescribed. "But we won't be putting off the treatment for CMV." If I continue to mend, they'll send me home in a few days, he says.

※

My father arrives before lunch with daisies in a florist's vase. He puts them on my bedcart, beside the tray that was just delivered. When I can't stand the scent of my meal anymore, I lean forward to inhale the neutral odor of the flowers' bright centers. I think about pulling them out of the vase after lunch and clutching them to my chest like Ophelia going under. It might neutralize the other smells in the room: the conditioned air hissing through the vents, my half-washed body, the bleach and rough starch they use on the linens. Dad offers me a cookie he bought from the cafeteria, but I have to wave it away. I try to joke: "You know your time is running out when you can't stand the smell of chocolate."

"Not funny, son."

"Thank you for the daisies. They're nice. Palate-cleansing."

"I guess you need that for such a gourmet meal." He and Rich have settled into a rhythm. Dad comes about forty-five minutes before visiting hours in the morning, and the nurses never shoo him away. In case they do he has a speech ready, which features the phrase "very ill only son." He stays with me while I have lunch, then gets something for himself from the cafeteria. Rich comes in the afternoon, as soon as he can get away. He brings me my mail and messages from my office. In the evening I've had visits from a few friends, but in this condition I don't really want to see too many people.

Dad likes it when I give him things to do, because he can get a break from me for a little while, so today I send him down for frozen yogurt. He brings me the daily paper and magazines I still can't concentrate enough to read. He helps me into the clean clothes Rich sent, because the doctors say I can try getting dressed if I want. I think this is code from my insurers, who must want me discharged, to the doctors, who don't seem so sure. Jodie is beside herself, asking if she should hop on the first plane and come up. "Stay put," I tell her. "Believe me, I'm getting great care." The last thing I need is more anxiety.

"You all through, son?" My father rolls the tray away from me and helps me lie down. He fills the blue foot tub with warm water and a few drops of the antifungal soap the hospital uses. He drapes a towel and wash rag over his shoulder and comes back with my shaving kit and the basin. "Let's sit you up just a minute so I can get this behind your neck for when we drip."

I wag my finger at his bare hands. "Dad. Gloves."

"Well, *I'm* not going to shave you, for crying out loud."

"You're handling my things."

"Oh, all right." He pulls on translucent green gloves and dips his hands into the basin. "I *could* shave you, you know," he says. "I was an unofficial barber in the army. Bet you didn't know that."

"I didn't."

"Made back most of the money I lost at poker every night, shaving the guys, giving them haircuts." He keeps one wet hand outstretched until finally I hand him the razor.

"This is a little weird, Dad."

"Well, I'm old now," he says. "I'm entitled to be eccentric." He squeezes out the shaving lotion from its tube, lathers my face in tiny circles. The smell of sandalwood and rubber makes a strange cocktail.

"Dad, did you feel a little, uh, funny when you did this for guys you didn't know?"

"Funny? Buster, I'm not crazy about boys liking boys, but I've been around those things plenty. Especially in the army."

"Don't I know it."

"All these years I definitely hoped you'd somehow snap out of it. The experience of true partnership with a woman, the experience of being a father, is a joy I can't just transmit to you in words."

I hope he won't try. "You seem to like Rich."

"Oh, yes, of course. Very much." He covers my other cheek. "Do you mind if I ask . . . ?"

"He didn't give it to me."

1990

"Oh. Good. Good. How long do you want your sideburns?"

"A little longer." He smooths the razor down to my jawline, then starts again beside it. He stands and bends to get at the other side of my face with the blade. "I still talk to your mother," he says. "I ask her things all the time, around the house and such. And about you, and Jodie." After he finishes shaving me, he offers me the mirror. But I don't need to look. I know what I look like by now, when I am clean shaven, and I remember what I looked like only last fall.

"You can't plan ahead for who you fall in love with, I guess, for the right person for you, I guess," Dad says gently. "I like Rich. He stands by you." He pours out the soapy water and settles down in the sticky vinyl chair to read. I doze, and when I wake up he is at the window, watching the sky turn auburn. I close my eyes again so he will think I'm still asleep. I feel someone's knuckles brush across my forehead, and when I open my eyes it's just me in the room. I push the hospital sheets off my chest and legs to enjoy the fading sun and imagine myself on the patio at home, or on the roof of my old apartment, or sunbathing at the Masonic Temple with Henry, knowing even with my eyes closed that he is looking at me, that other boys walking by us are looking too, that I am beautiful and belong there between the paws of a sphinx.

The sunlight is a substance in my room, gelled, buoyant, and slightly tickling. The room is so cool that I might be suspended in a lemon Jell-O shot with vodka. I might be someplace I'd really like to be. In a dark bar again, younger, stupid, with a second chance to go home alone, just that once, just those dozen times. The music is loud and the smoke is thick. My companion offers me a tiny paper cup, like the kind the nurses use here to dispense medications. I open my lips to let the sun slide down my unhealed throat, effortlessly sweet and hot. I know if I went back again in time, my choice would be the same. I would still say yes.

※

The tube is threaded through an artery above my heart and back out in a graceful loop below my left nipple. Three times a day one end of the loop is connected to a dose of gancyclovir by Claire, the visiting nurse. Once a day an anticoagulant is administered, which sends a flush of heat and leaves an ache over my heart. If I turn my head, I pull painfully at the stitches in my neck, or sometimes one of the loops snags on my T-shirt. The nurse also flushes the catheter with distilled water now and again, a thrill.

They tell me I can go about my ordinary life with this whole works. The nurse will teach me how to administer each dose. So I can lead a normal life, they say.

Dad doesn't want to go back to Dallas, but he has to, tomorrow. Rich wants to stop work on the house, but I won't let him. Henry offers to come a few evenings and do things for us. We grudgingly accept. I see how tired Rich is already. Alice says she can drop groceries by twice a week, and she'll drop off work too if I am up to doing anything at home. Other friends are starting to simply show up with meals. But it isn't enough. I think we are running out of something no one else can supply: time. We have to make do with what is left to us.

I read a newspaper account of a little boy who is positive for HIV. "I feel normal," he insists. Most days, during the day, I feel normal too, even with a direct line from the world into my heart. I'd feel especially normal if I could go back to work, calling estimators to readjust materials specs, walking the empty corridors of the Courtland Arms with Marcia Zenk, seeking some click, some trick of light, that she and I could agree to follow, that would tell us how best to proceed. Sometimes, if I am not careful lately, my mind wanders into some unpleasant places, and I have to bring it back, walk it along with me in the here and now, however dim the light, however slim the possibilities.

But at night, I find it hard to drop off without taking a mental inventory of my body's latest betrayals. A hint of foot fungus? How's that bruise over my knee? Any progress on the rash that just keeps on? How's the jock itch? Chest feeling heavy again as it did last winter? Sometimes it comes through in Dr. Lerner's rapid-fire patter: *Throat okay? Hearing? How's the old eyesight?* I've done enough reading now that a dozen possible diagnoses spring to mind against my will.

Rich never used to give me enough room in bed. Even if he was fast asleep by the time I got upstairs, he always managed to throw a heavy leg over my hip and pin me in a little corner. Now that he can't sleep,

1990

he complains that I crowd him. "Your leg weighs a ton," he says. "Move over."

I push the covers aside and grab his old robe.

My father is snoring in the guest room. I let the weight of each foot settle completely before taking the next step down, each of the wooden stairs squeaking a different pitch, leaning into the wall so I won't topple to the first floor through the dead space where the railing should have stayed. Rich comes to the top of the landing.

"David? What are you doing? Come back to bed."

"This goddamned staircase is a catastrophe waiting to happen. This whole house is. We're up to here in sawdust. I wish we'd never started."

"You told me this is what you wanted."

"No. You told me this is what you wanted."

"David, you wanted it first, years ago."

"You can change your mind about what you want."

It's too dark to see his face. I try to picture his expression. "I wanted to work on it with you."

"Well, look around. This is our handiwork. I just don't think we made such a great team."

"What does that mean? Do you want to leave me?"

I don't answer.

"Or me to leave? Do you actually think I would leave?"

"Sometimes I think you should. Why would you stay for the rest of this?"

"Because I love you and I chose to be with you. Of course I would stay. Of course I would. Oh, please come here. Come here."

"Don't do me any favors."

"Ssh. Come on and come here. Come back to bed."

"What do you want, though, Rich, what do you really want?"

"For you to be well again, but barring that, I guess I want time. Good time."

Rich is a kind person, all our friends would agree. He likes to have a good time, but he isn't afraid of the bad. I see the future funneling to a point right before our faces, not unlike the dark on this landing, a dark my eyes still haven't adjusted to. "Is the moon out tonight?" I ask.

1990

"Why do you ask?"

I don't want this to be another conversation revolving around my body and its failures. I shrug and let him hold me, let him lead me back to our bed.

Memories are never what you'd expect. They surface when you aren't looking for them, and though you forget exactly when they happened and often what was said, the smallest details are for keeps. For example, from a dinner party in 1988, I now remember most of all the candlelight flickering off our black dinner plates. It was Rich's birthday. Somewhere toward the end of the meal, I pulled strands of wax from the candles and rolled them into balls in my palm, listening to the others talking. The next morning at breakfast I found Rich smiling at his place, and when I sat down to mine I saw he'd transformed the wax drippings into the petals of a perfect, tiny rose around a charred stem of burnt match, and left it on my plate.

"I wish you could be really happy," I tell him now. "I wish I still made you happy."

Another day, a year or so before that party, we sat in his car one evening just after we met. Before the test? It must have been, but I can't remember. What we had been doing that day, I can't remember. I just recall the warmth of the evening, and how he lifted his hand off the steering wheel after stopping the car and rested it in a soft fist on my headrest. We watched two men try to uproot a shrub in their yard, jerking and then going still like time-lapse photographs. The evening heat had a tinge of cool, the first hint of fall. "School day tomorrow," I said.

Rich smiled. I kissed him goodbye and went inside. My apartment was nearly dark, so I turned on the lamp by the living room window and stood watching the street until his car pulled away from the curb. I stayed watching out the window even after he'd gone. It must have been a Sunday. Even then maybe I knew that one day, now, today, it would feel dangerous for me to be alone. Even then, already, my body had entered the final phase of life. In this phase I would fall in love, find a job I liked and was good at, move in with my lover. Someday leave both. End of story. For me there are memories of other safe havens like that moment of gratitude, standing by the window knowing I loved

79

1990

and was loved in return. But there will be no future from which I can date the next phase of my life and say that the tough and terrible times are now over. There will be nothing after this suffering, because I will end when it does. My friends and family will reach such a day, though. Rich, too. They'll enjoy a deep guilty joy at surviving, a moment to look forward to life's next challenge. Then each of them will reach past the day into their own inevitable death-days, singular as their lives.

Every minute of that evening, I felt loved and knew that I loved. I stood by the lamp at the window rubbing at my new loneliness in a tired, happy way, the way I used to rub my feet in bed after a long day at the fair. I think that was the last best minute of my life. Thank God we can't see the future.

The year is nearly over, the house nearly finished, I am still in reasonable health. The housewarming party is tonight. And we've developed a leak that is ruining the new entryway floor.

Rich walks in the door when I am in the hallway putting down a roasting pan to catch the drips.

"What's this?"

"I don't know. I've shut off the water upstairs."

"Oh well," he says. "After all we've been through, what's one more thing?" It occurs to me that we might never really finish, that even though the house might look the way we planned, even though the neighbors are already complimenting our sunroom, even though the furniture downstairs is back where it belongs, underneath remains a chaos we tapped into when the first wall came down.

Sometimes that happens. I know of one house that never had a major problem in its ninety years, and probably would have gone on another fifty without major repair, but instead failed system for system in ten because it was "improved." Pacing our front hall, I feel sure our patched walls won't hold. We'll develop new leaks or electrical problems or drafts that slam doors in empty rooms. Maybe it'll happen in the middle of our fine party, with its floral arrangements from Good Earth, and its waiters milling among forty friends with tapas. Maybe we will all die under the debris, half-chewed morsels on our tongues, guests at a housewarming in Pompeii.

Henry is among the first to arrive, with an aggressively wrapped, large and lumpy gift, taped at every one of its many edges. Rich waves him in past me, along with the other guests coming up the walk.

"Now, I could give you the chronological tour, in order of ground-

1990

breaking, or the theme tour, organized along the lines of comfort, entertaining, and luxury," he announces.

"Give us the tour of the bar," says Henry. "Wait. Let me give you your gift first."

"What in the world is it?"

"For your new study." It's a floor-standing globe, the old kind girdled in a wooden brace. When I spin it, its brackish greens and browns blend to gold. "Beautiful," says Rich.

"Yep, and I touched it first, so it's mine." I mean it as a joke.

"I didn't know you had started a list," says Rich. "That ought to come in handy when we divide the property."

"Ha, ha, ha. The authentic ones are leather," says Henry. "They used to stuff them with horsehair."

The room is getting hot, and the doorbell downstairs rings again. "David!" Alice's voice comes clear up our new open staircase. "Great," I say. "Everybody from work is here early."

Rich pushes the globe so it spins away from him. He doesn't say anything for a while, just watches the continents revolve from day to night. "Look, this even has monsters in the oceans," Henry says.

"Well. I should greet our new guests, and I could use a drink," I say. "Could anyone else use a drink?"

Downstairs our front curtains are open. A stranger passing, attracted by the lights, might stop to watch the room filling with friends. My boss, Meg, and her husband wave at me from the line for food. I make the universal gesture for someone who will be right back, pointing my index finger heavenward.

In the kitchen a boy—another of those duck-fluffy blonds that always seemed to bartend at our parties—has filled a metal bowl with crushed ice and lined up the brand liquors from tallest to smallest in groups of type. I point at the gin and vodka group. He makes my gin and ginger strong, because he knows it is my house. I slip behind him, taking my time getting past, to fish my cigarettes out from deep in the freezer.

The rooms continue to fill. Mainly I smoke. Others are smoking too, holdouts from the old days in spite of dire warnings. I find a place to sit alone on the brand-new back steps of the sunroom, ashing in one of the

1990

crystal goblets someone emptied and left there. The goblets belonged to Rich's grandmother and were supposed to be off-limits to the party, so it could only be a close friend who knew where they were kept.

"Somehow I knew I would find you out here."

Rich stands above me, holding out a small plate of sausages and cold pasta with gorgonzola, all too heavy for me to eat anymore. I tuck the glass back behind the flagstones of the new fireplace and shake my head at the food. "Why aren't you in there soaking up compliments for this masterpiece?" I ask.

"Why aren't you?"

"I'm tired."

"Is that why you haven't said more than ten words to me all night?"

I light another cigarette from the old one.

"You're determined to kill yourself, aren't you, David?"

"I have help."

"You guys, there you are!" Alice leans in the doorway, cheeks flushed. "Everybody is looking for you. Caroline and Tammy want the grand tour before they go."

Rich turns his palm up to show me off. "David will do the honors this time."

"No thanks. I'll just follow along to keep you honest."

"Fine. We'll start here, then. Alice, tell everybody we will begin at the beginning."

About five friends crowd in the doorway. "This film has more than two reels, kids," I announce. "So go to the bathroom now. But not the upstairs one, please."

"Well, come in, come in. You can't see anything from there," Rich says. "This is the first thing we started with. This room David designed from scratch." He looks at me expectantly, and when I don't say anything, after a moment he prompts me, like a child.

"Well, David?"

"What?"

"I thought you might want to comment on the process you took to sketch out our ideas."

"It was arduous," I offer.

"Ah. Thank you. It was arduous." Rich turns to our audience. "He

1990

says it was arduous. Not being a designer myself, I found it fun. It was nice to get a glimpse inside the process, and I had a very patient guide." This drew an appreciative "awww" from our listeners, as if Rich is just the most swell guy of all for being so big about the whole thing.

"Here, the fireplace is built so you can actually barbecue—see the rack back there. We have the VCR in the front room now, but eventually all that stuff will be back here."

"Making it all the more vulnerable to burglars," I say. "By the way, the barbecue was my idea."

"David, how about if you give this tour?"

"No, no. You're doing fine." We have collected other guests as we've gone along, until now there are more than a dozen.

"Let's go in. I'll show you the kitchen—copyright David—or do I need to? I think you see what it's like now, since you have been able to hang out in there."

"Well, not tonight," says Alice, "'cause of the bartender. But do have us back."

"The staircase was David's idea too. Right, David?"

"It's beautiful," breathed Caroline. "I think this is my favorite."

"I would never do it again," I say. "It's a hazard."

"You all go on ahead upstairs, we'll be right up," says Rich. "Go ahead." He pulls me into the handy space under the stairs, which I never realized was an argument nook. "How much have you had to drink tonight?"

"Excuse me? I'm kidding around and you're going to bite my head off in front our guests?"

"You're being hostile. Just humor me, please, this one night. If you can't enjoy the house with me, just be here, be nice if that's at all possible, and when everyone goes home you can let me have it, okay?"

"What would I let you have it about?"

"I don't know, David. Just whatever is on your mind at the moment, I suppose."

He's up the stairs ahead of me before I can say anything.

A man I have never seen before is crouching in our study, running his hands along the seam joining wall to floor. "Mmm, baseboard heating. Does it work?"

1990

"You mean the concept, or the offbrand our contractor chose?" I interject.

"The contractor was David's idea." Rich motions for everyone to come out and flips off the light while I am still in the room. "This is our bedroom," I hear him announce, to appreciative noises from our audience.

"I'll do this one, if you don't mind, sweetie," I interrupt from the hallway. "An instructive case study for anyone considering a bedroom skylight: Don't. Not unless you are willing to go all the way, as originally specified, and not skimp at the last minute because you are squeamish about the bottom line. Do you notice anything unusual about the furniture? Let me give you a hint: the bed is meant to be under the spectacular skylight. Why might it not be? Anyone—"

"David, I've never known anybody for pointing out their own flaws so quickly," says Henry.

"Oh, he doesn't do that," says Rich, still trying to laugh. "He'd never point out his own flaws."

"Darling, that's what I married you for."

"Oh come on," says Alice. "This is turning into . . . who is that guy who writes that mean stuff about couples?"

"The field is crowded," I say. "There is a lot of material."

Rich's face is nearly off-red. "David, you think you can just say whatever you please to me, about me, in private, in public—don't you?"

"So do you."

"No. No. It's different. You provoke me. You do it again and again. You deliberately push my buttons. You know how to do it."

"I'm not doing anything."

"You don't think you are. You think you can just remove yourself from us and play it the way you like it."

"What? Who's 'us'? What is that supposed to mean?"

"You know."

"No, I don't know."

"Guys! Remember us? We have to go." Alice pushes into the space between us, her mouth set in a straight line.

"Well, go then."

85

1990

She narrows her eyes and opens her mouth, but nothing comes out right away. "We can't go until you show us where our coats are."

"Find your own fucking coats." I think I enunciate clearly. "All of you can find your own coats. I am done playing host."

"That's what I mean! That is exactly what I mean!" Rich shouts. "You think you don't have to play by the rules. And I do. I always do. I have to play for both of us now. All the time. I have to play even better than before. How dare you do this to me, David. How dare you."

In just a minute he'll be sobbing, and I will soothe him again, apologizing as I have ever since we've known each other. I have no energy for this, but still I will do it. It will give me something to do, something familiar to say, as one by one our friends fade downstairs and out the door.

In bed that night, I tell him I'd like to go home for the holidays. "My Dad asked me to bring you down, too. What do you think? Do you want to go?"

"I think," Rich slows down to choose his words carefully. "Maybe you should go on your own again this time."

"Maybe."

"I think it'd be good for us both. It's been awfully intense, with the house and everything."

"I suppose. What happens if I get sick?"

"Are you planning to?"

"Thanks."

"I'm sorry. No, I am. I just mean, look. I don't want to leave the city right now. If you want to postpone the trip, I'll go with you. If not, then why don't you go see your family on your own?"

"Maybe I will." I turn away from him before he can turn from me. It doesn't take much for me to fall into a deep, innocent sleep these days. Even when Rich and I are fighting, which is most of the time.

There's a dream I have pretty often now. I lift off, flying from the roof of my apartment, bend my knees deep, and push up through the balls of my feet until I am airborne. I put my arms out stiffly, but then discover I can fold them against my body like an otter and streak through the air. It's the same dream, but I get better each time, dipping and swaying above an idling police van whose cherry light pulses

1990

across me, soaring over the couples who disappear into restaurants, the embers of their cigarettes briskly tracing their movements. I kick my feet to pick up velocity, coasting over Dupont Circle and just managing to avoid collision with the Lancaster Building. Over the little park I used to watch from my window, a woman in a sari and a young nanny in shorts look after the last three children in the early evening air. I turn back up to fly over Rock Creek, through the tall tree branches that smell of chlorophyll and car exhaust and the pollen of the tree of heaven. I am flying much lower now, but I see the shapes of a whole new place, the grid very like Washington's, with perpendicular streets crossed by diagonal avenues that meet in circles and squares. I can coast in close enough to make out smudged figures: a street cleaner with his cart of brooms, a jogger platt-platting along the sidewalk, families gathered on AstroTurf-covered stoops to watch their children skip rope. Then I'm flying over my old elementary school, and I see a little boy on the swing set who must be me, pushing forward with a fierce expression, swinging back with his face tilted to the sky. I inhale deeply and lift away from the furious little me in the swing, away from the school building. My sister—running across the lawn, a pack of boys in hot pursuit—falls away from me as I leave the earth. I could keep going, up and up, until I leave the atmosphere and burn in space.

On my way to Dad's from the airport, I roll the window down on the last few blocks, past the Christmas lights and dead lawns of my old neighborhood. We pull into the driveway.

"He still awake?" I ask my sister.

"Oh, you bet. Like this one." Jodie indicates Gina in the back, singing softly to herself in her car seat. "I'll come in for a minute, okay?"

I rap on the patio window. Dad is sitting at the table with his cup of instant coffee, holding his glasses away from his face to read the paper.

"Buster! Come on in. Come in. You must be so tired. Let me see you. Son, you look tired."

"Thanks, Dad. By the way, when are you going to get bifocals?"

"These are bifocals. My eyes are just shot. I'm serious. Have you lost weight? Jodie, does he look like he's lost weight?" I pretend not to catch Jodie's look before she shrugs.

Dad steps back to let me into the familiar kitchen that still smells of cooking oil and lemon furniture polish, as if Mom is bustling just out of sight. "Buster, are you hungry?"

"I ate on the plane."

"I picked up some deli from Wall's, just in case. It's in the fridge. You always liked Wall's."

"I ate on the plane."

Jodie and Dad both look older than I remembered. They move quietly in and out through the white swinging door to the kitchen.

"How was your trip, son? How's work?" Dad puts out bottled dressings on the lazy Susan. Catalina, French, and Thousand Island in a mayonnaise jar, the name jotted on a white label in his handwriting instead of Mom's.

"Fine. Fine." I acccept the plate of fresh salad and cold cuts, both

1990

strictly off my diet. He sits in his customary place, his shadow moving against the white tablecloth where Mom's plate would be. "How's Cal, Jodie?"

"Fine. He'll take Gina for a few hours if you want to do anything tomorrow. I have some shopping to finish. You want to come?"

"Sure."

"Call me when you get up. Get some sleep."

When Dad and I are alone, he watches me pick from my plate, smiling only when I look at him.

"David, son? Aren't you hungry?"

"Fine, Dad. Just a long day."

Most of the time whenever I talk to him he seems the same as before, although around Mom's birthday one year he surprised me with an angry phone call, furious that I hadn't remembered. I didn't know if he expected a call, or a card, or maybe even a present, something Mom might have liked. I kept saying to him: Tell me what you want and I will give it to you. But I couldn't give him what he wanted, because he wanted Mom.

Tonight I lie in my old room at the far end of the house, listening to the joists settle and pop as they always have, terrifying me when I was young. The bare branches of the pecan tree, planted when we moved in, are tall enough now to carve through the outside light, filling the room with shadows. I catch the scent of mildew creeping into the walls and just the hint of a drowned rattle at the bottom of my lungs.

My parents' room is all the way across the house, with Jodie's old room directly across from them. My room is—was—across the living room, through the shadowy kitchen, just beside the garage. This house, like the one near the airport, has a hall whose length was pure terror at night. I visited my parents' room with bad dreams and stomach aches more often than Jodie. I was sure no other boy at school was such a baby. In order to save some of my pride, I brought my pillow and blanket in with me and slept on the floor at the foot of their bed instead of crawling in with them. I listened to my mother's light breathing and the occasional snore from my father. Sometimes one or the other of them murmured in their sleep. The clock ticked through the night, the hour changing with a sharp click. If I were truly sick, I

1990

knew, I could wake my mother simply by standing by her side of the bed and saying, once, "Mom." Her blue eyes snapped open like a doll's when she heard my voice.

The next morning Dad sits across from me at the kitchen table, cocking his head over the empty lazy Susan. "Buster, know what I found when I was cleaning up the garage?"

I'm on my second cup of coffee, the real stuff I was smart enough to bring with me this time. I feel a bit better.

"Buster?"

"Sorry, Dad. What'd you find?"

"Wait right here. I'll show you." He slips out of the kitchen in his Hush Puppies, opening the garage door so I get a whiff of mold and wet from the garage subfloor. He comes back with a shirt box from Joske's, a store long since gone.

"Look." He pulls off the lid and shows me a jumbled city of pasteboard inside.

"Silltown! Dad, I had completely forgotten."

"Your mom told me once she was saving them for Gina, but I only just found the box today."

"Oh, these are so old. Let me make Gina new ones."

"What do you mean, old? This is the original Silltown!"

"Well, this will be the historic downtown, then. But I'll make some new ones too."

At some point, maybe around age ten, I began to make miniature buildings my mother displayed on the kitchen windowsills. At first there were just a few pioneer houses in the shadows of ivy plants and diffenbachia. Soon I'd branched out into building generic business complexes and skyscrapers. Eventually we cleared two entire sills of vegetation and gave them over to a one-street city.

"Your mom said she knew you would do great things when you started making these," says Dad.

I squeeze his shoulders, afraid I might topple over if I move too fast. Sometimes I get sick after I've taken my morning meds, and if I ignore it, it goes away. In the car with Jodie, I try not to focus on the endless gaping intersections we speed through to get to the newest and biggest stores. It's a familiar route, but it looks all wrong. Things aren't where

I expect them to be, and there are new things where nothing once was. Jodie says, "Look how built up it's getting out here. There's the old school. See? Behind that huge health club? You could almost miss it."

I half expect to see small faces pressed against the glass, watching the traffic go by. But the windows only reflect gray light. The yard is packed with metal portables for more classes. At the edge near the fence are the old stand of pecan trees and the swing set you could always find me on at every recess, while other boys played tetherball on the blacktop or climbed the jungle gym I used to draw. I stayed on the swings, tipping back my head to the blank blue sky, legs pumping me higher until the chains sang with a high yellow sound, and gave a hitch and a clank at the top.

"It's about like I remembered."

"Really?" Jodie leans over the steering wheel to get a better look. "Everything seems different to me."

The longer I stayed on the swing, the more my thoughts stretched out so I could think them each at a time. One idea led to the next like the links in the swing chain. Creak and whine, creak and whine, back and forth in layered rhythms.

Once a boy at the top of the jungle gym cupped his hands and shouted, "Faggot plays with girls! Faggot plays with girls!"

I ignored him. Somebody had to be faggot every day, and it wasn't always me. I had to hope Jodie wouldn't overhear, or else I'd see her standing near the jungle gym, quivering and alert, demanding apologies.

"F-a-a-a-ggot!"

Jodie marched over to the jungle gym and stood at its feet, glaring up at the offending boy. "Say that again and I'll fix you good."

I stayed put in the swing, letting the buzzing, clanking hum block out everything else for a few more minutes. The trees loomed close, receded. The minute I slowed down and stepped off, all the thoughts would coil back around themselves, the one on top bugging me to go over there and fight for myself.

It's when I sailed out over the playground that it felt the best, with the hard-packed ground so far beneath me I could do nothing but be where I was. When I nearly touched the dusty hollow made by all the

1990

other feet before mine, I tucked my legs and swung back, with a sick thrill at the thought I might crash backwards through the sagging metal fence. Each time I swung close to the ground I thought, this time I'll keep my feet down, this time I'll skid to a stop and get off. But each time, something else in me tucked up again.

"Look at him. Scared!"

"Hey faggot!"

"Shut up! Shut up, shut up!" Jodie was almost crying. I wished she wouldn't cave in like that. I wished she wouldn't come over here at all. We still had a long time before the bell would ring, and once I was off the swing I couldn't go back. I'd probably spend the rest of recess circling some other boy, trying to avoid his punches while a crowd gathered.

I could hear them all making fun of Jodie now. Pretty soon they'd trap her on the ground if I didn't go over. When I reached the farthest point behind me and began to sail down again, I prepared to unfist my hands. It was easy to keep flying once I jumped, elbows cocked as if I still gripped the chains. My feet flattened on the patchy grass, sending a shock up my spine. The place between my eyes tingled.

One of the girls, who got off when I did, asked if I was all right. I started walking, my knees ready to go in a different direction from the rest of me, like the plastic giraffe on Jodie's dresser, with a button at the bottom to make its limbs crumple, showing the thin elastic that held them together. "Leave my sister alone," I said.

"Leave my sister al-o-o-one," said Mark Reilly, and all the other boys started in too, clasping their hands and weakening their knees even though I stood straight. "Leave her alo-o-o-one, leave her alo-o-one," they chanted, until Reilly said, "You gonna make me, faggot?"

"Yeah, I'm gonna make you." I held my arms loose, away from my sides the way my Dad showed me. *Leave your hands open until the other guy fists up, but don't let his friends pin you.*

"How you gonna do it, punk? Punk? Huh? How you gonna make me?" Reilly leaned in and started to tap my face with his fingers, little short prods. I promised myself this time I would do what I'd been taught, put up with it and never take my eyes off him, until I thought he was comfortable, then I'd connect. *Don't screw around. Go for the nose, go for the stomach. Nothing below the belt.*

1990

I tried to watch him and my back at the same time, but Jodie was all around me like static, pleading for us to stop. I tried to think her away. Then someone got both my arms and Reilly was in, getting me in all the places I was supposed to protect. Stomach, head, stomach again. *Fight fair*, said my dad. All I had free were my legs, and I was kicking but I couldn't get a purchase on the ground. Reilly was dancing in to take his turn and dancing out to give someone else a chance. There was something tasty and dangerous in my mouth, and when I saw Reilly's spattered knuckles I realized I was spitting blood. Next time I put my head down and butted as hard as I could, then swung back and butted the boy behind me. I know I caused damage, but not enough for anyone to let me go or stop until the bell finally rang. The boy holding me dropped me while almost all the other boys, including Reilly, scattered to pick up their lunchboxes and make themselves scarce.

Jodie stayed on the ground with me, sobbing and helping me look for my lucky rabbit's foot, which came off my belt loop and somehow disappeared. "I'm sorry," she said.

"Shut up. Just be quiet."

I had to clean my cut lip in the stinking boys' room, watching my back all the time. By the time I got to geography the teacher had already drawn down the map of the world. I can't remember what she said to me when I took my seat. Instead of the map I examined my hands. The dirt had washed away easily, but the blood that crusted in the crevices of my palms and fingers stained a tiny star like an asterisk that rested on what I thought was my lifeline. The star darkened from brown to black when I began to close my hand.

※

At the mall we walk from store to store, stopping at nearly every window, which lets me rest and sometimes close my eyes without her noticing. I want to believe it's only the crowd, or the shouts of all the children begging for things they can't have, and all the parents who are the reason they can't have them. I feel dizzy and glassy at the brightly lit perfume counters, limp and heavy in the food court with its baking cookies, pizza, and grease. We stop to sit near the crowded mall bathrooms that smell of used diapers and disinfectant. Bags and children

93

1990

are everywhere underfoot. There is too much of everything we don't need, and of the things we need, too little.

I let the bags I've been carrying for Jodie rest at my feet and grab her to keep my balance as I sit. I try to explain that it's only the crowds, all the confusion. But I have to stop talking and just close my eyes. That helps for a few minutes, and then the spinning intensifies like drunkenness.

"It's all right." I open my eyes again. "Just give me a minute."

"I'm ready to leave if you want."

"Jodie."

"What?"

"Do I look bad to you?"

She tucks her arms around herself and stares between her feet. Soon her shoulders begin to quiver and her head bows onto her chest. "I'm sorry," she whispers.

"No. No. Ssh." I gather her to me, unsure she wants me to. I feel just like I did on the playground, snatching my rabbit's foot back and trying to sort out who was worse off, who was sorriest. "Come here."

She locks her hands around my neck and leans into me the way Gina does when she wants to be carried. But Jodie doesn't want to be carried. She wants to stop carrying me.

※

Julio's was where a bunch of us went on Sundays for years. Alice, sometimes her boyfriend Joe, Brian, Henry, Gary, me, and then Rich.

"Hey," said Brian that Sunday half a dozen years or so ago, "Sweetie, how are you, you look *good*." He was losing his lover, and every time I saw him he wanted to engage me in deep discussion about my survival issues. One time I pissed him off because I told him I didn't think survival even *was* an issue.

"Cool sunglasses, Alice," I said. She tilted her face up for me to kiss, her eyes behind bright, opaque blue ovals that mirrored my distorted face, making her seem distant and ethereal, a contemptuous angel. "Let me try them on." I modeled them for Rich, who nodded his head, and Alice shrugged. "They're *me*," she said, taking them back.

Joe said, "The waiter comes by every half hour whether you need him to or not." He pursed his lips and reached for the pack of cigarettes I'd taken out of my shirt pocket. "Glad some of us still smoke," he said.

"Well, my frame of reference is a little different from yours." He ignored my comment and helped himself to my lighter too. The fluid flickered in its transparent green body, the flame shooting too high.

"Hey Henry," I said. "Where's my drink?"

"You were late, child."

"You knew we were coming. And you know what I like."

"Oooh. Evidently not as well as some." Henry gave Rich an arch look. "What made you guys so late anyway?"

"I was waxing my legs," I say. My friends observed a tidy silence in Rich's honor. I knew what worried them — whether, and how, I would "behave safely." I looped my ankle around Rich's under the table, my arm through his above it. "Fuck it, I can't drink any more anyway. One drink makes me want to puke."

Henry was already back to reading the Sunday *Post* over Joe's shoulder. "Boring news," Henry said. "All of it's old." He pointed to one headline after another. "This is old, this is old. The only new thing is this. That yacht team that took the America's Cup. What's it doing on page one anyway?"

"It's new," said Joe.

Alice cocked her head at me and smiled to deepen her one dimple. "Your color is nice," she said. "You been getting more sun?"

"Not exactly. Probably just liver trouble."

Now Henry was arguing with Brian about why people were so fastidious about dress and manners in previous centuries, when they were so casual now.

"Now that we have plumbing," said Henry, "we can afford distance from our own animal processes, so we don't have to be courtly."

"So, like, when we had chamber pots and outhouses we had better manners?"

"Right, because we had to rise above the shit, so to speak."

"Uh-huh."

"Pizza." The waiter was back with a couple of trays. Henry started in on him immediately: "Some of us *still* don't have our drinks." The waiter took one look at Henry and served the other end of the table first.

1990

"I disagree," said Brian. "I think people had these elaborate codes of manners because otherwise someone was liable to murder someone at the drop of a hat."

"Well. But that doesn't stand up to scrutiny, because that's true now, but people aren't acting out these elaborate customs."

"What, so the goal is to find a unifying theory for why customs are relaxed now?"

"Yeah."

"Maybe they're not. Here." Brian took a handful of paper napkins from the waiter and began to hand them around. "Maybe they're just as elaborate but they're second nature, so people don't realize." He put the remaining handful of napkins, far more than we'd ever need, in the center of the table.

"You think that when people were memorizing handkerchief and fan positions and leaving calling cards they weren't aware of it?"

"There's a whole other issue here," broke in Alice, "which is that history typically documents the behavior of the ruling class, people with a *lot* of free time on their hands. I doubt that people in the slums of London were leaving cards for each other."

"Can I ask a question here? Who is eating meat and who isn't?" Joe held a plate aloft, ready to serve.

"Wait," I said. "You people are getting your eras all compressed. You started out in chivalry and now you're into the Age of Reason."

"Plus, that's a fraction of the world," said Rich. "We could start talking about Africa or Asia and the whole history would be different."

"Well, who knows anything about *that*?"

"Who knows anything about what we *are* discussing?"

We spent afternoons like these talking ourselves into a fever pitch, becoming slowly drunker, resorting to other forms of expression as the day wore on, singing or telling loud jokes or sneaking off, especially if the straights left early, to screw around in the john or at each other's apartments.

We worked our way around to evolution, and why gays exist.

"To get to the other side."

"I've been reading *Seth Speaks*," said Brian, "and he says that gays are a stabilizing force in society, whether anyone admits it or not. We have to look at this thing systemwide. Balance. Promiscuous men and women among the heterosexuals are like a wild card, stirring up the gene pool. So are bisexuals."

"You've been reading *Seth Speaks*? Define 'read.'"

Rich broke in loudly: "There ain't no such thing as a bisexual, honey; that is the oldest story in the world." I'd found out, by this time, that he was a predictable type: closeted when sober, but sassy and even capable of a scene after he'd had a few.

"Oh, I beg to differ," said Brian right back.

"Maybe men," offered Alice, "being xys, carry their ambivalent chromosomes around with them. Maybe men are the carriers, and as long as there are men there will be gay men. Women on the other hand, if you follow my logic, being xxs, carry with them a natural affinity for each other. They love each other because they can drop all pretense when they are alone. They call each other sister affectionately."

"Amen, sister-breeder," said Caroline.

"Whereas we crave that tension and indecision of the man drawn to a man," I continued. "I get it. We only call each other brother at protests!"

"Where's Gary already?" asked Henry. "Wasn't he supposed to be here?" Alice shrugged. "Well, I'm going to go call him." He stood up, bumping the chair of the person behind him.

"Buy me cigarettes?" I wheedled.

"You shouldn't smoke so much," he said.

"Fuck you, I'll get them myself. Hey—" I pointed to the street and Rich's eyes followed mine. "Look over the edge here, see that green car? Now watch." I leaned as far over the ledge as I could go, mustered up a mouthful of saliva, and spit a clean arc that, if we'd been close enough, could have been heard to ping on the car's shiny roof.

"Impressive," said Rich. "You like to see things fly off roofs, do you?"

"Impressive, yes, that a grown man would bother to hone such a skill," added Brian.

"I do like to see things fly. Since I was a wee boy," I replied proudly. But not everyone at the table was laughing. Brian and Alice shook their heads at me, as if I should know better. When had they become the

1990

arbiters of maturity? If they didn't let up I'd run down to the street and scrawl with my finger on the dirt of that stranger's car: "Spit on by a PWA."

"Gary's not coming," Henry said, coming back from the payphone.

"Is he okay?"

"No. He's not. I'm going over there."

"Henry—"

"Shut up! I'm going. How much do I owe?"

When his face was like this, pink at the temples and as if he might cry, I felt like he was looking through me. He hated that I wasn't the one going over, not today, not ever if I could help it, hated that I was positive too and yet could sit here with my new boyfriend, asking for cigarettes and maintaining my complacency. I remembered this same expression on Henry's face many times in college, when he was still trying to make me love him, and it hadn't returned until Gary got sick. When Henry told me to find my own apartment, I wasn't completely surprised. He said that I permanently confused him, permanently. He said I was his best friend but even better at a safe distance. But he felt that way about so many people. By then I was ready to move in with Rich. Rich took most things in stride, had never looked back once he was committed to me. I didn't ask why, and he didn't offer to tell me. We just stayed together, day in, day out.

"Forget it." I draped my arm over Rich's shoulders and looked Henry right in the eye. "I'll stand you this time. You can owe me."

My first night home with Rich again, after Dallas, I lie on my back in the dark watching the clouds cross the moon. I tilt my head back so the crown of my skull is almost on the pillow, taking in the upside-down perspective of the Kleenex box, tissue flapping like a flag, the cup of cold coffee from that morning or before, the half-full water glass, magnifying part of the title on a paperback copy of *I Ching*.

I keep thinking about the one-street city. My mother sat at the kitchen table behind me as I worked on a new tableau. She hummed softly to the radio or sometimes talked to friends who called her, stretching the long beige cord of the phone over to the kitchen table so she could be with me. I pointed out the highlights, taking her on a waist-high tour of her windowsill.

See, this is the stadium, and this is the church. Here is the elementary school, and here is our house. There's the temple, and there is the cemetery.

I wonder what my family is doing now. Jodie, Cal, and Gina in their quiet weeknight house, where a phone wouldn't ring except for an emergency. I wonder what my dad is reading, and if the creaking of the house unsettles him. Is Henry sleeping alone or is he out tonight at the bars? Maybe he's up fretting about me. By two o'clock I've moved on to people I don't even know, proxies for me out in the world having fun, like the tired kids breakfasting at Au Pied de Cochon, sweat drying on them from a night at Tracks. There are millions of PWAs—what is the count up to now?—too many, with peeling or patchy faces, every color of skin, shifting symptoms, living and dying in houses and apartments and beds in shelters and makeshift camps on streets and, of course, often, in crisp costly beds smelling of machinery. And in my lover's bed.

1990

"I think it's not enough," I say aloud.

"What's not?" So he is still awake, after all.

"Just to stay together. Just because I'm sick. I mean, if it's just about kindness."

"It isn't just about kindness."

"But it mostly is."

Rich sighs. "I don't know."

The next day the sidewalks are glassy, slick silver. We linger in the house all morning, out of things to say. In late afternoon, we slip along on this improbable pavement toward his car at the curb. A sharp wind picks up from the east, scraping my face with a thousand pins. When the ice is this new, it is almost too beautiful to matter that it is dangerous. By tomorrow it will be a little safer, more visible when heel prints pock it and dirt clods mottle its surface. It will be sanded here and salted there by worried merchants, managers, owners.

Rich is a good sport to take me ice skating, of all things I insisted on today. I want to do something outside, something physical that lets me coast. The Ellipse is warm from all the people skating, so I unzip my jacket and Rich pockets his scarf. For the first new moments, we struggle hand in hand across the unevenly shaved surface. The single evening star hovers under a thinner slice of moon than last night.

My eyes are already smarting from staring at the bright blade cuts beneath us. "I feel I should warn you," I tell Rich. "I can't stop looking at my feet."

"Oh, you should really look up," he says. "It's such a beautiful night." He squeezes my hand, and I almost lose my balance.

A rosy-cheeked girl in pink tights and a checkered sweater slices past me. She claims the rink's center, unlike the other children, who can manage only a few long passes before they veer and slap against the flimsy guardwall. One boy clings to the rim. When his feet slip from under him, he nearly sits in a split on the ice. "Laugh at it, just laugh," says his mother. He picks himself up, but he can't laugh. Rich lets go of my hand and goes ahead.

The girl in the pink tights stays centered, carving a figure eight over and over into the ice. Her eyes are blank as she mouths the counts to herself. Across the way I see Rich, making his way steadily through the blur of others, both ahead of me and behind me in our tight circle.

The girl bells into a wide curve, swinging her arms across herself and back in a dreamy mimic of the eights inscribed in the ice, nipping into the figure's slim waist at dead center and out again in a mirror curve. I throw my own arms wide for balance, trying to catch Rich's eye. He never sees me. We each skate on our own in the circle, swimming through the breath-laden air.

Slow, slow, slow. I nearly stop. My ankles adjust and readjust over the slender blades that connect them to the ice. There is a zen to catching yourself before you slip and to knowing when it's too late and you can't avoid crumpling. It has to do with balancing your weight, back and forth, to transform the part of you that would make you fall so it becomes the base for new balance. You bend your knees and center yourself. To stop in emergencies, there's always the acceptable cheat: Veer into the fence at top speed and cling to its lip as your feet go out from under.

It's been a while since I skated, and although I manage to stay up the whole time, after less than a half hour I'm winded, with a chill burning in my thighs and ankles. I push myself, but I start to get dizzy. I have to ask Rich to take me home. He coasts off the ice and sits beside me as I unlace. This is the way it goes now. We can still get the outlines of our good times down, we just can't fill them in.

"You want dinner? We could go out for a change." My friend, he wants to put the best face on it, as if he is ready to go and as if I am hungry. We both seem to feel that strange happiness, relief, that comes when a breakup starts to be real.

"Sure." I would rather go home. But it doesn't matter, so long as I stay with him for now.

The clouds block all but the bright star, Venus, and the chilly winter moon. We hold hands again, unsteady on solid ground because we're accustomed to ice.

1990

※

After dinner I find him upstairs in the bathroom, drawing a bath in the newly enameled clawfoot tub. As if I am not even here, he unbuckles his pants and drops his other clothes on the floor behind him. He eases into the hot water, his back to me. He's planning a long soak, I see. Lit candles and incense burn on the white wood washstand.

"You're welcome to come in," he says wearily, when he sees I won't be leaving the room.

"No. It's okay." I feel foolish in the doorway. Usually it's been Rich who persists until the silence abates. "I'd like to stay for a little while longer, though."

"Suit yourself." He immerses himself to his chin, ears just above the surface, breath rippling the water, and fixes his gaze on the opposite wall. I go to my knees beside the tub and rest my chin on its metal rim. "I had a good time with you today," I begin. "I like it that we can still have a good time together."

"Yes. Me too."

"There's so little that matters enough to fight about."

He hands me the washcloth he's been trailing in the bath water. "Here," he says, not unkindly. "Make yourself useful."

He's there with me for just that moment, his eyes on mine, his lips forming again to speak, then relaxing as he thinks better of it and leans forward so I can wash his back. I soap the cloth liberally the way he likes it and sweep his back with suds, circling over his spine and shoulders, then ease him back to lie belly up. I bring my hand, still covered by the soapy washcloth, under the water. I settle my palm gently over his groin. He is half hard already from the warmth of the tub. The water rocks my hand gently, making it seem as if we have all the time in the world. He closes his eyes and relents. This small bathroom, that seemed at first so cold and hostile when I stood in the doorway watching him prepare for his bath, now enfolds us both in candlelight and time. He lifts his hips and I use both hands now, one over the other, bringing him close and then stopping, close again and then stopping again. He covers the amulet drain with his foot so the water won't seep out. His likes his baths deep. With a sudden jerk of the legs and a half-hearted cry, he comes. I take my hands away. My back and knees ache, and we rest. Neither of us speaks.

"I really do think it's best that we split up," I say, finally. "Don't you?"

"Probably, yes. Okay." He stands. I offer him a towel and a hand to get out.

※

I had a letter all written the week my mother died. And an overdue birthday gift, wrapped and ready, all but given. It was Jodie's suggestion: a hand-held electric fan. "For when she gets short of breath like she does," she said. How was I to know how it went? How was I, over a thousand miles away, to observe her dying habits?

"She just . . . nothing she does now is like anything she'd do before," said Jodie. "Even when she does things she'd do, they're not."

I pressed for an example, something we could name.

"Well, she doesn't talk when we watch TV. You remember how we used to always have to shut her up? Last week we rented a really stupid movie, some Clint Eastwood road picture, one of those funny ones with the chimpanzee, she likes him so much. She was so quiet we thought she'd gone to sleep. I turned around and she was still staring at the tube. With this look on her face. I thought she was thinking of something terrible, but then there was a punch line and she tipped her chin back a little. She was laughing. She didn't move her mouth. Just a little nod. And that stare. But she was laughing."

I thought of the word the death experts use. *Withdrawal.* I imagined my mother crouching back into her skull as the pictures crossed the screen, until they seemed to recede from her. Like when you look out the back windshield as a kid, and the house seems to move away, when in fact it is you who are leaving.

"All the things they can do now," my father said when my mother persisted in dying. "All the wonderful things. They're doing everything they can for her." At the end of her life they were giving her a dozen varieties of shiny new capsules and tablets. "And it's still not enough."

Later he confessed that she asked him to shoot her one morning. She wasn't sleeping by then, and neither was he. Each night he locked his arms around her as if to prevent her from slipping away. He knew he was waiting too long to take her to the hospital. At first she wouldn't go, and then he couldn't stand to bring her. She was increasingly silent, until those moments when, my father said, she seemed to want to jump out of her skin, sitting with a start and spastically jerking her hands over her body, choking for breath.

"She woke me at five or so. She told me I ought to buy a gun," he said. "She told me if I loved her enough I would shoot her." When he said no, she stopped speaking altogether. She refused food and water. She turned from him in bed at night, brushing his hands away weakly, too tired to act more decisively but just strong enough—he thought— to signal her contempt for him, for his unwillingness to give up his need of her.

The morning they called me to tell me she'd died, I sat at the kitchen table, turning and turning the empty glass pitcher with a white ring from the water it held at dinner the night before. Then I stared at the one red Fiestaware platter from my grandmother's house, in mint condition beside the crystal goblets that belonged to Rich's grandmother, in the cabinet near the dining room window. Six pale green Depression glasses, bought at an estate sale when I was in college, lined the wall behind the spice rack. An entire set of red china complete with gilded shepherds and shepherdesses, a weird inheritance from my godmother, Letty, gathered dust in our attic. These things had come to be here from people I knew or were bought from strangers now gone. Rich and I displayed them together instead of wedding gifts, our mutual ties to the dead the firmest bond to each other we could demonstrate, the permanence of certain objects representing our marriage.

My mother's last word, I suppose, was "no." That's what was relayed to me by my father, who was told so by the nurse who found my mom, after Dad had just gone down to the cafeteria for a minute. Apparently she tried to get out of bed herself, and the nurse found her on the floor in heart failure. I heard versions of the story repeated by family and friends. Days later, it was extending through the filaments of the family network, into the world a thousand ways.

"Her last words were, 'No, I don't need your help.'"

"She saw the damn life support equipment and she said, 'No.'"

1990

"She was fighting for her very life, her very life. And even when she knew she'd die, she said, 'No!' But it was too late."

"That's just like her. What a fighter."

"... the very thing you have to say if you don't have that Living Will. She said 'I refuse life support.'"

"She said, 'No help.' Just as stubborn—"

"She simply said no."

"Simple."

"Not so simple."

"We'll never know what she said, really."

"Yes."

※

Right before their wedding, my parents were caught in a home movie, practicing the waltz in my grandmother's garden in late summer. Dad found the projector and set it up in the living room after dinner sometimes, so we could watch again. There was no sound, but I could almost hear the voices of the cicadas that would have been weaving in and out in the trees, their mantra punctuated by the hacking falsetto of the mockingbird, two icy notes slicing the heat.

My mother's father, still alive then, ran the camera. When my dad set up the movie, we watched them practice a clumsy box step on the flagstones of the patio, barely missing the heavy bushes, once, then twice. On the third time my father pulls my mother back with him and they both lose their balance. The tired petals fly around them. We laugh because we have seen this before.

My mother never drops the relentless smile with which she weathered every family crisis over the decades. She pulls my father back out of the thorns, smiling at the camera all the while. Now our dad backs up the movie and moves it forward a second time, and a third, just to make us laugh. The dancers mince once, twice, then off the path completely and into the bushes. Dad pulls them out again. He puts them back on the flagstone path, then backs them up and dumps them in. He pulls them out, he backs them in. They are just as surprised every time.

We know it's a trick, but still we are surprised too, hoping over and over that they will see it coming this time. The camera shakes as my

1990

grandfather moves toward them. The rest of the garden falls out of frame: the driveway, the neighbors' house and mailbox, the rosebushes along the walk. My parents face the camera, collapsing their formal dance frame to throw their arms around each other's neck.

The earlier frames have played and replayed so much I've lost the thread of time. This could be taking place before my parents fell or after. I tense up to see which way the film will go, but it's a circle now, and whatever is coming could as easily take place in the past. When you dance, someone always goes backward. My mother could see the rosebushes over my father's shoulder, but she wasn't yet good enough to warn him. All she knew was that it was her part to follow, smiling, even when they fell. My father seemed more at ease going back, as if he preferred not to see what came next. He is like that now, too, rewinding the film all the way back again, back again and back.

※

Nowadays my doctor is sending me all over town, having my spleen checked, my feet, my skin. Henry pulls into the circular drive of Georgetown Medical Center—which apparently has the best spleen people—to drop me off. The weather has turned, taking on an amber, summery cast. Even so early in the day, it sharpens the shadows collecting around the building's footprint. I hesitate at the entrance, close enough to the glass doors to make them slide open on their electric tracks, exhaling a cool antiseptic breath from the hall. A nurse nips in ahead of me and slips between a pair of neat-coated residents coming out from inside, her jacket flaps spreading behind her as she moves from sun to shadow.

Little red stars have appeared on my arms and chest, pinpricks as bright as fresh blood. They unite in constellations near my arm joints and across my stomach. They were all right as long as I could hide them under collars and sleeves and slacks. But then they spread to the backs of my hands, under my jaw, and now my face. The dermatologist tells me it's folliculitis: wherever I have hair, there it could spread. He prescribes a topical ointment and still another antibiotic, urging me to keep the rash exposed to the air. But I can only work with the things I can hide.

1990

I leave an empty chair between me and a man reading *Newsweek*. The patient next to him sits rigidly, staring at the opposite wall with both hands folded over his crotch. The only other person in the waiting room looks nervous. His handlebar mustache and tight white Wranglers mark him for a throwback to the '70s. A man in his fifties comes out from behind the mauve door to the inner office, carrying a yellow windbreaker and smiling. The nervous man in white jeans stands as if he's gotten an electric prod, cracks each knuckle in turn, and joins the other man to check out at the glass reception window.

The *Newsweek* reader next to me turns to a full-page photo of carnage, another conflict already two weeks older in the Middle East, all olive drab and red flesh. He tips the page toward me while he scans the article, and the light from overhead bounces off the glossy picture. I wonder about the state of the cleanup in that country, how long and in what weather the dead lay before they were put to rest. The two men at the window murmur with the receptionist over some billing problem.

The door to the inner office opens on its brisk hinges. "Mr. Carlson?" The young technician with her clipboard stands aside for the man next to me. The mauve door shuts behind him with an efficient two-pat click, leaving only me, the nervous crotch-protector, and the quietly arguing couple at the desk.

I'll get used to this waiting room too, I guess. Like most such places, it's designed to be inoffensive. The walls are wheat-colored tweed, and the expensive carpet has worn badly near the office entrance. The door hangs too low in the frame, snags the rug every time it's opened. If the waiting room were darkened, you could probably see a thin slice of light at the top of the door, perhaps only an eighth of an inch.

Henry comes through the badly hung door, but he doesn't sit down. He stands over me, jiggling a leg nervously. "I'm going to get a Coke," he says after half a minute. "Do you want something?"

"I don't think so, thanks." Henry nods with relief and goes.

The couple at the window is still hassling with the receptionist. Finally she lifts her voice above their protests. "I'm sorry. You'll need to get us the paperwork from your last employer before we can file this claim. Or you can pay now and have your new insurance reimburse you." The two roll their eyes at each other, and one of them produces a credit card, while the other collects the folder full of paper they brought, which apparently wasn't enough.

Henry comes back with his soda, pops it open with a short spray, and smiles at the scowling couple as they go. The man across from us burrows his palms still deeper between his thighs. He looks reasonable enough; if someone were to point out to him he is clutching his crotch, I bet he would stop. That someone will not be me, however. I watch Henry neatly lick the spray from the top of his open can.

He stares back at me. "What?"

"I'm sorry," I say. "That's just so unsafe."

"Oh, I know," Henry agrees. "One of these days I'm going to slice my lip open."

"No, I mean the germs."

He looks the can over for a moment as though he will see the germs there, then moves the discarded *Newsweek* to sit down.

The door opens and the technician beckons me in. "Doctor's running late," she says.

"That's okay. I don't have to be anyplace else." Behind me the other man is asking how much longer he has to wait.

After we're done Henry takes me to a place in Georgetown where they sell cosmetics for men. The clerk takes one look at my face and stays behind the counter. She hands Henry samples and disposable puffs so he can do all the work.

"We have this whole line now of powder bases," says the clerk from across the glass. Henry stands back in a forced posture of envy. "God, look at you, I am jealous. You don't have any of those tiny wrinkles I do."

"And I likely never will." The clerk looks appalled.

Then it is on to the Safeway on 17th Street. "What do you think we should pick up, David?"

"Depends what you have at your house."

"David, we just had this whole conversation five minutes ago in the car. Nothing. I said I have nothing."

"All right, all right."

"Sorry. It's been a stressful day." He hands me the basket as I follow him up an aisle. All around us stroll ordinary, only slightly troubled

1990

people, pushing their baskets among the shelves full of soup, home remedies, and snacks. I'm sure Henry doesn't want to hear again, even if I could explain this time, how I like to pretend I feel the beating of ordinary hearts around me when I go out now, reassuring voices repeating dull little troubles sotto voce beneath the piped-in music, how every now and then I pick up pure joy, like static spiking and fading in my inner ear. The bodies of these ultrasound creatures scour the orderly shelves, selecting hummus or bean dip, brussels sprouts you hardly ever see fresh anymore, gold and red peppers for too much money, candy and magazines at the last minute. I miss this even though I'm still doing it. I miss how easy it is when you can't imagine it changing. Their minds can be elsewhere, while mine is right here, compulsively soaking in every detail, from the fluorescent light that chatters in the highlights of our hair to the mottling of the D'Anjou pears Henry picks out. One, two, three, he hefts each one gently in his freckled hand, nestles them in our red basket, the stem of one poking through the plastic lattice.

"I never noticed you don't bag your stuff either," I say. "Rich never bags his stuff. Maybe you two have a future together."

"Yes, there's the basis for a lifelong commitment. How is Rich these days?" We're in line to check out. Henry hands his money to the cashier and waits for change.

"You know we're splitting up."

"Yeah, I sort of talked to him about it last week." That's all Henry says. I wait for him to launch into me, not here but on the street or in the safety of his home, about "getting help," about "sticking with it," about going back to take fuller advantage of Rich's amazing kindness and boundless patience. But Henry only seems to be paying half attention. The other friends are after me all the time now. Brian keeps writing down the name of someone he sees for therapy. Alice has made phone calls, done her homework on my behalf: "It's called 'PWA Alive!' They meet at the Church of the Savior on Tuesdays. And they have outings too."

"Outings, how nice," I said. "Who of?"

The sky has cleared to a dark blue that edges the buildings with neon. I'm already tired, but I dread the night, tossing in our bed alone,

1990

waking up to hear Rich wandering from room to room below. It's a simplification, but not untrue, to say that I feel him waiting for me to leave.

"I'm looking for a place," I say. "Cheap as possible without being too cheap. If you hear of anything."

Henry doesn't answer.

I look at the old botanical prints of fruit and vegetables in Henry's kitchen, the ones he's had since college, each a drawing of a whole specimen and a section cut away so you can see the inside, with leaves and seeds suspended beside them in neutral space. My favorite is the plum called Tragedy. Its skin is dusty violet, the flesh a pinched, sickish yellow. The illustrator thoughtfully rendered the blight on one of its furled leaves, the lacy gnawings of aphids. One overripe plum is pictured falling an inch from a branch into the nothing of the background. "You know, it's funny the things I'm so used to that I don't even look at them anymore. How long has it been since you really looked at these?"

"I don't know," he says, with only an edge of patience left in his voice.

"What?"

"Forget it. Let's just try to salvage the evening. Here, rinse these."

"What? Rich? You're mad at me about him."

"No. You have your reasons, I'm sure."

I see so much in the simplest things, I just want to look and look. Then I also want to stop. How the salad greens resemble shirred ears, how the porcelain sink is like the one in my mother's kitchen, how the smell of pasta steam reminds me of cooking with Rich when things were still good. Lack of sleep, I'm sure, malnourishment, yes, or something more insidious. A new symptom. An overloaded ocular nerve, humming with heat, about to snap. Misfired synapses, breaking circuits, an upset neuron throwing a tantrum. But wouldn't I be forgetting, then, wouldn't I see less? Maybe it's just me, trying to listen and look and remember everything, everything, everything.

"David."

"What? I'm sorry, what?"

Henry sighs dramatically and reaches across me to turn off the tap.

1990

"You were washing the lettuce in hot water. Come sit down." He pours wine into both our glasses.

"You just don't know what it was like, Henry. Take my word for it. He was trying too hard. It was embarrassing, it was too sad. I just didn't . . . we didn't . . . we didn't love each other anymore. In a sane situation we would have simply split up, no big deal. Aren't I still entitled to that? And Rich, the poor man, isn't he entitled to be let off the hook?"

"I'm not buying this somehow. I don't know why, but I just don't buy it."

"Buy it or not, I'm not going back. I was suffocating. He was suffocating. I mean, how can I . . . look, he wouldn't ever leave me, you know, I did him the favor—"

"Okay—"

"So I . . . how can I permit him to waste his life this way?"

"It's okay, it's okay."

"How can I submit to that? How can I know I did that to him? I'd rather go home to my sister and father. They want me to come home. Or check into a hospice. People should be thanking me. Rich should be thanking me. I mean whatever love was left, I chose to let it survive. Don't you get it?"

"I get it, I get it. But it's so stupid. David, it's suicide. How are you going to live on your own now? Why in the world are you looking for an apartment?"

"That's patronizing. I have a job, you know. I have great prospects." I'm laughing at that one, we both are, and then both crying.

"Forget it, then. Drop that topic," says Henry. "On to the next."

"Here it comes."

"Support group. You need one. You do, David. You do."

Sometimes the shadow passes over me and I imagine that I will be dead one day, within the year, within the month, I don't know when. I try to imagine the fluids congealing in me, the flesh setting, the cold creeping in. I imagine my spent body being buried or being burned. In fact I must decide soon, or must I? Tick tick tick. Isn't this the wrong attitude, aren't I giving in really, giving up? The magazines say we shouldn't be labeled victims or sufferers. We are survivors. But I do not feel like I, in particular, am surviving. Anyway, I can hardly stand to be around any of the other *survivors* for long, much less a roomful, to the constant disappointment of my nonsurvivor mates who seek support for me. I always despised group activities. Why, now, at this late date, should I seek the pleasure of meeting people with whom I have little else than a pathology in common?

※

"One type of load is really dangerous because it has dynamic impacts that increase progressively over time. Anyone."
"Resonance."
"And what is resonance?"
"It's a force rhythmically applied with the same period as the structure. Like a wind that peaks cyclically exactly every ten seconds."
"Right. Unlike in life, in architecture you literally do not want to be on the same wavelength. That's like music and glass: Hit the same frequency, and the glass will shatter in seconds."

※

So on a Tuesday evening a few weeks later, Henry and I arrive arm in arm at a meeting of PWA Alive! Jiri, the leader, is a small man with a thin mustache. From what I can gather he is either an early case or an empathetic seronegative. He ticks off the things he did that week, and his list is invitingly bland, the highlight being the visit to the DMV to register his car. "And so another week for me, alive!" There are nods of approval and even applause from the circle of ten. I dart a glance at Henry, who stares forward noncommittally.

The agenda for tonight is to cover our goals. We are given pads of paper and pencils if we didn't bring them, and we are asked to make a list. I consider suggesting that we work on our obits instead, get those out of the way, but I figure I'll be a good sport this one night. No one else looks happy doing this either. A few of us write busily; others chew on their pencils or dash off an item or two and then wait. Jiri sits back with his arms crossed, calling, "Five minutes. One minute, time." Henry is still writing, and I stopped long ago.

"You didn't have to participate, you know," I whisper savagely. "Seronegs don't need well-defined goals."

1990

"Very funny," he says. "I didn't want to stand out."

"Who wants to go first?" Jiri doesn't have to wait long before someone raises his hand, a young blond with nearly transparent boils clustered on his elbows and neck.

"Balance my checkbook," he reads. "See about filing for disability." He stops for a minute, takes a deep breath, starts to read but stops again, then starts again. "Uh, write to my folks. Keep my appointments."

"That's fine."

"There's more—"

"Those are good, Michael. Good. Someone else? How about, pick your top two goals."

Now a timid man about my age starts in: "Plan a trip. Eat more balanced meals."

"Excellent. Excellent! Who else?"

Henry gestures for me to raise my hand. I shake my head, but Jiri's eyes flicker across me. "You want to share tonight?"

I think of the most outrageous thing I can say. "I should get my will in order."

No one else looks shocked. "That is a big task. Maybe you could break it down?"

"What do you mean?"

"Well, have you talked to a lawyer? Listed all your assets? Some other people here have wills you might want to look at, for models. That sort of thing. It's great that you're facing this head on, I should say. What about short-term goals?"

"Getting through the day."

Jiri laughs. "We'll work on that." He moves on as if I also said I would plan an exciting trip or improve my nutrition. Even Henry just looks at his watch.

※

The entire two top floors of the Courtland Arms are finally empty now, and others so lifeless they might as well be. Taped to the wall beside the elevator is a small white note neatly written in blue ink: "Elevator is shaking. Please be careful off-and-on." A few apartments have been unrented for a year by now, but most were more recently vacated,

1990

some so recently the management hasn't even cleaned yet. Hair and nail parings seem to grow in tufts between the bathroom tiles. The floors bear weight marks from removed furniture, and the ghosts of family pictures checker the walls. I walk across the bare wood in each stuffy apartment to hear the echoing of empty space, and sit where a person might sleep in the bedroom, my head against the windowsill. When a truck passes on the street below, a vibration shimmers through my bones. I like to know the old building is responding to stress, bringing all its hidden joints into play to reestablish equilibrium.

1991

Now I live in that future I couldn't see, in a small apartment at the edge of 13th Street. I painted the living room walls a blue called Aegean, took up the orange carpet, and whitewashed the scarred oak floors. I rented this place for its cheapness, because I can't work much longer, but I chose it for its three-windowed bay, so like the one in the old house.

My godmother once lived nearby, in a rooming house for ladies on Logan Circle. A girlhood friend of my mother's, she worked for Kennedy and then Johnson, but years and strangers divide us from being neighbors. She died before I came here to live. She sent me birthday cards and U.S. savings bonds from One Logan Circle, Washington, D.C., and paid a rare visit to my parents' house in Dallas the summer I was thirteen. I remember opening the door to a stranger recognizable only from photos, a short, slim woman who enfolded me—not like other female relatives who squeezed me or shuttled my nose into their dress fronts, but as if to balance me like a large, expensive package she wanted to set down. Then she smoothed past, trailing Chanel and a red suitcase on wheels, tossing her gloves and purse on the table in one gesture.

She and my mother screamed when they saw each other, and sat for hours in the kitchen smoking and drinking iced tea while I stood by quietly, trying not to kick the table. My godmother insisted I call her Letty, not Aunt Letty or Miss. She asked me all about school and my friends, and then my mother asked me to show Letty the guest room.

The room was actually Jodie's. We were far too old to share, but we did for the week that Letty stayed. I lifted the red suitcase onto my sister's bed and turned to go, when Letty put a hand on my arm and told me she had a gift for me and my sister.

1991

In her red suitcase was a book called *Washington, D.C.: The Story of Our Nation's Capital*. She watched me turn the pages, both of us sitting on the bed, the suitcase between us open to her unfamiliar clothes still under tight bands. The inside cover showed an old drawing of an unfinished city on a swelling river, dwarfed by a rectangular building.

"That's the Capitol before the dome was built," said Letty, taking off her shoes and rubbing the hooded heel and toe of one stockinged foot. "Where the Congress works. At night, when the light at the top of the dome is lit, it means they're in there, making laws."

But I wasn't looking at the Capitol. I was looking at the handful of broad avenues splaying beyond it, bisected by smaller streets. Sometimes they met in stars like the lines on a hand. Barns and houses and grand buildings lay practically next to each other, and to the left the drawing smudged out into trees and farmland. In this small place was everything and nothing at once: a wilderness, a river, farms and factories, churches and railroads, the seat of government and houses with little patchwork gardens.

"Look at it now," said Letty, showing a map in the back of the book. The trees and farms were gone, the little streets crisscrossed everywhere, and the avenues were marked with names of states.

"This is where I used to live," said Letty. "On Rhode Island." She showed me Logan Circle on the map, one of the stars where streets and avenues met. "It was nice once, but then there was everything."

She didn't tell me what everything was, that it hadn't been safe to walk near 14th Street after dark since Dr. King was killed, since glass and fire had spilled into the streets.

So I joined the ranks of people who fell in love with Washington without knowing a thing about D.C., drawn to the federal city by stories of greatness expressed through the magnificent white buildings that were dreamed, aborted, and then reborn, without knowing anything about the millions of red bricks that make the real city, the buildings pulled down in their prime and the others living long beyond expectations. Only the early map of lost farms and little houses reminded me that something else might be there. Letty, who loved the stories of places too, told me what she knew about what was lost or still could be found: the few remaining old Victorian markets where they sold vegetables and meat on Saturdays, the wild strip of burlesque clubs on Bladensburg Road, the river park called Rock Creek, where she'd once been canoeing. And the most terrible thing about a building I'd ever heard, before or since: how the Knickerbocker fell in the Blizzard of '22, on the heads of nine hundred moviegoers cuddled in the dark.

Such details often worked against themselves to improve desire, at the age I was then. I wanted to live in just such a place of grand disasters, instead of Texas, with its tornadoes and rough thunderstorms. Snow was different, cold and soft and elegantly menacing. Years later, when I saw a picture of the Knickerbocker, I felt a sick thrill of validation. It looked like a cake that had been iced too soon, its roof collapsed but its standing walls still perfect, even to the festoons and fancy lightworks. Its Greek style would strike you as odd for a movie palace unless you knew the shadowed temples it was meant to emulate, like the ones I wait in front of for my bus downtown, the palaces of science, statehood, Masons.

※

A bank stands on the old Knickerbocker site now, in Adams Morgan, where Henry and I shared an apartment just out of college, right before I met Rich. On Saturdays there is an outdoor market there. To get the best produce you have to arrive by eight. That day I think about often, the day I met Rich, I was there around noon.

I got a flat of herbs for our kitchen windowsill and some nectarines from a vendor I felt sorry for, always at his table in the shadow of the bank. Most people avoided his eyes on their way to the cash machine, even if they had to stop right in front of him to rest their packages or untangle their dogs from a frenzy of socializing. His wares were always so thin, spread on a checked tablecloth instead of heaped in bins like the other farms' offerings. He'd have two baskets of berries, a couple of eggplants, a few nectarines, two buckets of carnations. There was never a sign on his table, and he never spoke to me. It could be he was only selling what he pilfered from the others. I took my chances.

The Knickerbocker fell in a blizzard year, when the tiles became waterlogged and a seam opened in the ceiling. After the crash, there was a silence none of the survivors ever forgot. Ninety-eight people had died in a wink, but a few deaths fanned out over decades. The architect gassed himself in his apartment four years after his name was cleared. The roof contractor was killed on a job, his mind elsewhere. The owner shot himself in the '50s. Another theater flourished on the site, then died of old age, and the bank took over. Life went on.

That guy at the market could never keep his change straight. He counted carefully, shook his head, took it all back and started over. If he was even my age I'd be surprised. But when he smiled, his teeth showed black roots.

My old professor Van Lare would find the chief attractions on 18th Street too low to suit him, I think. The buildings are ordinary, brick commercial flats circa 1910. They're remarkable only because of their tenants, restaurants from every corner of the world up against each other, tricked out with red doors and bright blue awnings, painted with fanciful scenes like those on the walls of the cafes Fourchette and Lautrec, Saigonnais and Montego Bay. Nothing much has changed in the years since I lived there. The street still smells of spice and oil; the sidewalks are thronged almost every night. By day you feel as if you're near the river, although it's more than an hour's walk. The pace is like a pleasant riverfront's, with people doing their shopping or looking in the antique stores. That morning a few couples were sharing breakfast at the cafe tables at Belmont Kitchen, wearing their jackets because it was still cold. I pushed open the door of the card store that's gone now, knocking the bell against the glass.

The shopkeeper said good morning without looking up. He was examining slides with another man, holding them up to the light one by one. "Valentine's Day items are all for sale," he said. I chose a stupid get-well card for Gary, who had flu. The card was one of those full-color photos so popular then, a gaggle of queens in horn-rimmed glasses and prom gowns smothering a shirtless young hunk in kisses. This one had a nautical theme. *What do you give the man who's got everything? A wide berth. Hope you're in full trim soon.*

I cut up Belmont on my favorite route home, past the old Victorian houses whose round bays bellied up to the sidewalk. I had the street to myself, except for two roofers on a town house, bowing their knees to the tiles, sloughing them off and pitching them over the gutters to the

1991

ground. Every so often, scabs of red tile fell and smashed in the street, but traffic was sparse and no one got hurt.

Henry wasn't home when I got back. I put my flat of herbs on the table in the sun and made a pot of coffee, glad to be alone. My old terra cotta plant pots were waiting, pulled out of the hallway closet and piled in the sink. I mixed vinegar, water, and a few drops of bleach in the sink to soak the pots the way my mom taught me always to do. These were pots I hadn't used since Henry and I left Charlottesville. Pulling them apart, clearing away the cobwebs and clinging peat moss, running hot water over them, I was back on our wide front porch that last year of school, planting herbs there. Now I remember remembering in that kitchen on Columbia Road. Standing by Henry's bright chrome and red Formica table, with the smell of bleach flaring my nostrils.

When Henry came home he always asked, "Who's here?" as if there'd be anybody but me. Sometimes there was.

"In the kitchen." I pulled on my rubber gloves. He squeezed past me and opened the refrigerator. "Guess who I saw?" he asked.

"I don't know, but you're right in my way."

"Sorry. You're in mine. Gary."

"Oh. Is he better?"

"Hardly. He looks like shit. He says hello."

I dipped my sponge in the water and squeezed out the excess. "What's he doing up if he's not any better?"

"I think he has it." Henry came and stood by me, drinking calmly from our water bottle.

"No way," I said.

"I wish. When I saw him, he was standing at the Safeway looking at his list like he'd been there for hours. Like he's in shock."

From the kitchen window, I watched people weave back and forth under the temporary awnings on the bank plaza. "I think you're jumping to conclusions."

"Whatever, but I'm going to get the test."

"Oh, come on."

"I'm not kidding. You should, too. Get it over with. What are you doing?"

"Planting things."

121

1991

He brushed his hands over the rosemary on the table and put his fingers against his face to smell. I rinsed the sink, filled it again. From so high up you could even see the Church of Christ Scientist a block from us. They used it as a temporary morgue the night the Knickerbocker caved. People still worship there as far as I know, and of course they mourn. But they have never since trafficked in the dead at such a volume in one day.

I drained the old water, and began filling the sink again. "Is Gary well enough to come to the party tonight?"

"He said so."

We were lucky to be young. Because we could have this conversation and then go on, me to finish up in the sink and open the bag of potting soil and fill the pots around the new little root clumps, Henry to get out the vacuum and crank up the stereo and bring our few chairs into a circle for the party. I got out the camera sometime that afternoon and took a photograph that I now have on my refrigerator, of Henry collapsed on the couch with a scarf tied on his head, the vacuum still upright beside him. The day a seam opened over our heads.

※

I cut a photograph from the newspaper this year, in January when the Knickerbocker disaster had its anniversary. It shows the theater on the day after, its heavy façade still intact all along 18th Street, the snow already almost gone. I like that if you ignore the roof, you wouldn't know what happened. I like that the architect's walls held up, the bad joke Van Lare might have made of the odds. *Probability is not a meaningful concept when four out of five elements stand, but the one that falls is the roof.* But the plain fact is that many more people would have died if the whole structure had collapsed. Didn't that mean anything to the architect? Wasn't that worth surviving?

On second thought, it made no difference to be young. Because what else do you do but go on? What have I been doing since then but going about the small rounds of the day, and what do I have to show for it but photographs and canceled checks?

Alice brought Rich to meet me at our party that night. He kept offering to help in the kitchen, and between that and his tight, tiny smile

1991

I felt sorry for him. "Kind of you to offer, but as you see there's hardly room to turn around," I said, handing him two six-packs of beer, hoping to flush him out into the main room with a purpose.

"How do you know Alice and Joe?" he persisted. I had to admit I liked Rich's open, smoky voice and the slight pressure he put on *d*'s and *k*'s that told me he was from somewhere near, but not too near, New York City. I tilted my head and took a better look at him.

"Alice and I went to school together, and then we worked together."

"Oh, so you're an architect."

"Right. But where we worked together was a restaurant. She moved on, I haven't. So to be accurate, I'm supposed to be an architect."

"Ah." Rich lifted his arm away from the refrigerator so I could slip a jar of olives back in. It wasn't a particularly muscular arm, but when he held it over my head like that, I felt protected, blessed. He had kind of a rabbinical profile, heavy in the jowls, with a dark shadow of new stubble on a recently shaved face. "And what do you do for money?" I asked.

"International development, at a nonprofit. I'm an economist, if you really want to know."

"I'll bet you could tell me everything about externalities."

He laughed, showing a set of extra-sharp canines. "What do you want to know?"

"What do you want to tell me?" There it was, the shift of the feet to bring our faces closer. I leaned the small of my back against the sink. "All I know is that it all comes down to money."

"Not so," he insisted. "Anything but." I took a beer out of one of the six-packs he'd left sitting on the sideboard. I noticed Alice in the doorway, not obviously eavesdropping, her hip turned out toward the party as she balanced her empty glass in her palm and stared at the floor.

"What's it about then?" I asked Rich. "You tell me."

"The consequences of decisions."

Alice tipped her chin at Rich and wiggled her eyebrows at me when he wasn't looking. I called her bluff. "So, Alice, what do you think it's all about?"

"What's what about?" she asked, innocent.

"Economics."

1991

"Don't know. But I have a good economist joke. Want to hear?" Just then, with a burst of greeting, Henry opened the door to another guest. Then suddenly the next room seemed too quiet.

"Excuse me a second." From the kitchen doorway I watched Gary make his way to the sofa. "I shouldn't be out at all," he said. "But I promise I'm not contagious." He still wore his hat and jacket, so sitting by the window he looked strange, poised to leave again even while he settled back against the cushions.

"Gary, I'm so glad you're here!" I offered. I went right to him, made myself lean over to kiss his cheek. He smelled rumpled and unwashed. His cheeks were blotchy. "What can I get you? A drink? Some tea?" That's how it would go from now on, for years offering friends a good time and a salve in the same breath.

"How many economists does it take to change a light bulb?" Alice was asking Rich. "One: to assume a ladder!"

"Honey," Joe said. "You mixed two jokes together. The light bulb joke is 'two: one to assume the change and the other to calculate its cost to society.'"

"What's the 'assume a ladder' one?"

"I think they fall down a well in that one," guessed Rich.

"Oh, well. It works my way too."

The room was warm, but still Gary stayed bundled, hands in lap, seemingly contented. Henry sat on the edge of the couch, pressing his lips together and not saying much.

"I'm sorry I don't know any architect jokes," said Rich.

"It's not a very funny profession," I assured him. "You build wrong, somebody probably dies, you know?"

"Or sues."

"Or both."

He followed me back and forth from kitchen to living room, which was filling with new people so fast we simply left the front door open after a while. The elevator was just across the way, so our party guests came in clumps, like refugees arriving at a way station. "What kind of architecture do you want to do?"

"Me, I don't know."

"How old are you, if you don't mind my asking?"

1991

"Twenty-five. I'm getting a late start."

He laughed. "When I was twenty-five I was still slogging away at the USDA, crunching numbers for milk subsidies. Life is competitive. If you really want to do something, you have to pay your dues." He made each statement a little more slowly and waited longer for my reply. He was standing so close to me now that it was hard to concentrate on anything but his scent, familiar beyond the warm wool of his sweater. "Architecture is also an art form, after all," he offered.

"I thought so when I started out. In school we read Vitruvius. Do you know him? He made this famous list of qualities necessary to the profession, sort of a Hippocratic Oath for architects. The highest expression of man's existence. I took it to heart. I even signed up for astronomy because it's on his list. But look around at what architects do, for the most part. They're not looking at the stars, that's for sure."

Gary grabbed my arm from where he sat. "Can we close the window? I'm freezing."

I don't like it when people grab me. At first, that's all it was. Gary must have seen resentment in my face, because he pulled back, just enough, and let go. Then I knew what I really wanted, and it wasn't pleasant. I wished he hadn't come at all if he couldn't be his old self. I wanted things to be easy again. I wanted Rich's attention all the more because it could distract me, but when I turned to him, he'd turned away, and whatever clever comment I was about to share withered on my tongue. I mixed with the others again, feeling as though I'd prepared for a fight never started or an accident narrowly missed, my breath just short of a gasp, blood surging, adrenaline burning a path to my heart.

※

I agreed to meet Rich at Dupont Circle about a month after that, stopping first at another card shop to buy more get-well wishes for other friends, and Rich was waiting for me outside the Metro, looking older than I remembered. In his pale trenchcoat and sober tie he seemed straighter, even a little square. I felt conspicuous in my checkered jacket from the thrift store, my pointy wingtip shoes. He switched his metal briefcase to the other hand when he saw me and stretched his

1991

free hand out to shake, very mid-America butch. "How's your week been?"

"Well, I've been applying for design jobs."

"No kidding."

"Yeah. This one place seems to really want me. They do residential projects and rehab enormous old buildings."

Rich chose a booth toward the back at Mr. Egan's and sat smoothing the red vinyl table covering with his strong hands, looking around while I talked. "They have a really terrific project just across the street," I prattled on. "In fact they invited me to the opening tomorrow night. Want to come as my guest?"

The waitress dropped off our drinks. Rich fell silent and pulled his hand away before I could touch it. I felt young and blundering. I didn't know the first thing about conducting a thoroughly private life, because I didn't bother. The way Rich looked around him on the street and took such care to pick a booth in here, the way he started and edged back whenever I leaned toward him, as if he was terrified I'd lunge for him. And I was about to. I saw myself as he must: the bleached hair and heavy baby face, the tiny gold loop in the left ear, the bolo tie and starched white shirt. I was so visibly queer it embarrassed him. But he was interested anyway. I resented his discretion.

We both stared into the table until I thought we'd bore holes. *Forget about this stiff,* I thought. After a decent interval of conversation I signaled for the bill.

"Are you in a hurry?" he asked.

"I just find this place kind of a bore. Why not go over to 17th Street with me?" Maybe he would loosen up in a more natural habitat. He insisted on paying, to which I gave a token protest. Out on the avenue, a silver charter bus whistled past us into the tunnel, under the circle.

"There's the Lancaster, the project I was telling you about." We stood across the street at the corner to get a good look at the ten floors layered with slender cast-iron columns. It's still there, of course, the tallest of half a dozen other grand old slices of pie that ring the circle. A cleaning crew moved from floor to floor, lighting up a row of windows all at once, darkening others. One man cleaned the smoky doors of the lobby, making the glass shiver each time he jumped up to reach the top.

"They put a garden on the top floor. Tomorrow night you could be up there sipping champagne."

Rich looked at his watch. I thought I was about to lose him. Later I would find out that was a habit, that Rich never felt safe unless he knew where he was in his day.

"Or why not tonight?" I heard myself saying. "I have a roof deck. We'll find a liquor store on the way. It's a nice evening."

"You want to?"

"Why not?"

Up on my building's roof, a cold breeze swept over us. We dragged two chairs from the pile near the door and sat at the railing, looking out over downtown and the glimmering, far-off monuments. I twisted the wire cage off the champagne's cork and torqued the bottle slowly, letting the pressure do its work. "Aerial views are magic, aren't they? Down there you see every crack, every failure, a bad building where a good one used to be or should have been. Then up here you have this pretty grid, the avenues slicing through just where they should, the circles and squares. God, what a beautiful place Washington is. I never planned to stay here, but I fell in love. You know what? I forgot glasses. I'll be right back."

"No, no. We'll just drink it like this." Rich turned the open bottle to his lips. "It feels more reckless. Are you still with him?"

"Who?"

"This guy you fell in love with."

"I'm not in love with anyone. I fell in love with the city. With Washington."

"Oh. Ha. Okay." He held the bottle above his head. "Let me toast your love of Washington."

"Let's toast love wherever it rears its ugly head."

"Hear, hear." He drank again and handed the bottle back. I don't like champagne, so I swung my arm over the railing edge and poured a dose on the street. "I christen these imperfect little streets the S.S. Majestical Grid."

1991

"Aren't you supposed to break the bottle?"

"I will if you want me to."

"No, no."

"I will." I held the bottle sideways to the railing, ready to smash, jetting a spurt of champagne over his trousers. "Now look what you made me do!"

He laughed but took the bottle away. "I've known you only a month and you're already trouble," he said.

I should have known then that one of us would always hold back. Him, then me. That's the way it is in any couple, healthy or sad. You can't both jump in together or who would keep an eye on the time? That night it was Rich watching the clock, maybe even when I finally kissed him, chastely, in the old-fashioned way I'd almost forgotten, just brushing his lips with my tongue.

※

"Why don't you just ask him if you're so worried about it?" asked Henry. "Or better yet, get tested together. It'll be a bonding experience."

"I bet." The Western Blot was all the rage that spring, but I didn't like to cave in to trends. "Anyway, I hear it doesn't do any good to know, because what's the point? We're being basically safe."

"Basically? It's the adverb that worries me."

"Well, it's a contradiction to go crazy with lust and keep your wits about you." I knew Henry's logic was good. If I asked Rich to test with me, it would simply seem a touching gesture of commitment. If he already knew he was positive, we would get it out of the way. Me, I was okay.

And in fact, it was a good idea, at least at first. Rich agreed to take the test, and then a funny thing happened. He began to fall in love in earnest, calling me at work each day, wooing me with little jokes and anecdotes. We went to the clinic after work one Wednesday, had a tense dinner at Boss Shepherds, went to his place together, and slept fitfully without making love. All the week that we waited, I noticed that even though I worked and talked and socialized as if all was well, a monotonous drone kept up in the back of my head: DoIDoesHeDoIDoesHeDoIDoesHeDoIDoesHe?

1991

"You're fine," said Henry. "Stop obsessing."

Wednesday night Rich and I held hands in the clinic waiting room. Rich emerged from his private conference with a big grin. We hugged and waited some more, and then I went in for mine. The counselor began, "I'm sorry..."

We walked back to my apartment the long way, from the dark blocks near the clinic to the festive corners of Dupont. There were people talking and laughing at the foot of the fountain, and the light from shops and passing cars had never seemed so creamy soft. In the summer evening the restaurants were brimming with people. A sidewalk vendor was set up at the traffic light, his pale gladioli and daisies glowing green, then amber, then red.

"Let me buy some flowers," said Rich. It was the first thing either of us had said for blocks. He took my hand, on a public corner, in front of strangers, knowing I was sick. I pointed out a bouquet of thick, heavy glads. I cradled them all the way home, holding my new lover's hand, feeling oddly safe now, feeling unseasonably happy.

※

For a long time, I could still be happy like that. My peace of mind rested on a whole new theory of existence constructed at a moment's notice but fortified and embellished over years. For a long time I was more content than I had been with ordinary actions, secure in the truth that since no one else knew how they would die, since in fact such ignorance is part of life, that I had been given an almost unfair intelligence, a better basis on which to plan, a more realistic horizon point. I had a keener sense of likelihood, and so I went about my business with rare gratitude. Also, I was in love, and he wasn't leaving.

That lasted for a while. Then I started reading the obituaries with an appetite for finding men as young as me, reading between the lines to see what killed them. I was looking, not for triumph or hope, but for fellowship. Soon enough over these years I've found friends, and friends of friends, and men I never knew but whose names I'd heard. Gary. Brian. Paul. Patrick. Michael. Beside their names, the names of living friends seem hollow and light, playing back on my message machine at the end of every blessedly ordinary day:

1991

"Where have you been? It's Alice."

"Hey, it's Henry. We missed you last week."

"David, this is Alice. Are you out of town?"

"Dave. Call me back, okay?"

There has come a time now when the day's first success is retrieving the morning paper, when the crowning glory of its passage is taking out my trash. My range of movement having telescoped, I crave the smallest, sanest acts: bending, lifting, picking up my feet, pulling open the door of the trash chute and pushing my bag through. As I get sicker and tireder, the smell of my garbage has changed, and I can't stand to keep it even overnight, with its medicinal bottles and empty tubes of cream for aches, its wasted frozen meals from friends, vegetables I've bought, then let go bad. Long after I have stopped taking care of myself properly, I insist on being the one to drag this bag of old man's trash out every night, pushing myself along against the walls of the short corridor, rattling with broken glass and good intentions.

I pull back the metal door and push my bag in. Tonight there comes a new feeling as I turn my back and hear my wasted things booming down through the gullet of the building. I've lost the slender thread of my theory. I understand that my disease gives me no special privilege. It is simply an accident, not only my infection, but my survival and its inevitable end. My disease is a fact; the exact time of death, a detail. A life form itself, the virus has stumbled by chance into my system, just looking to survive, and it will kill us both trying. It is as surely unaware of me as I once was of the universe, in which my childhood room was a mere tiny point.

❋

Van Lare demanded a lot of us. On the first day he chalked these words on the green board at the front of his classroom: *Structure (skeleton). Cladding (skin).* By the end of the second week we were theoretical masters of the logic of structural design. Types of load: static (dead and live) and dynamic. Other types of stresses: resonant and aerodynamic.

"Static loads. Baum."

"Loads you can plan for."

1991

"Like?"

"The structure itself."

"Very good. And that's a dead load or a live load?"

"Dead?"

"What would be a live static load, then? Not you, let's see, Marbry?"

"People?"

"Yes. Anything else? Take your time. Furniture is one. What distinguishes a live load from a dead one? Steiner."

"You can never measure precisely what the live load will be."

※

This one man, this one night, before I met Rich, about a year before that party, I remember lived way the hell at the end of the Yellow Metro line in Virginia, in a white carpeted condo in a tall white building, in a complex of identical buildings. He brought me back after last call at Tracks, pulled out his boyfriend's bathrobe and tossed it to me, saying, "Let's go down and swim." He wanted to let me know I was part of a routine. Maybe I'd picked myself a murderer to go to bed with for good. How would they find out? My body dumped somewhere? Or that I didn't come home, and it was clear I meant to, all my things left behind, clothes for tomorrow spread on the bed.

This guy took me down in the elevator to the basement where a warm laundry smell hung over the cement. "Out this way," he said, opening a heavy door the color of a gun.

He opened the gate by the pool with his magnetic card. I wanted him to go in first, but he motioned me ahead. We slid into the turquoise water on opposite sides and met at the floating line dividing the deep end from the shallow. When we kissed he dragged me across the line into his end, and the plastic rope dug into my chest. His hands grabbed mine underwater. If we slipped and I wanted to save myself, it'd be up to him to let me go. I tried to gauge which of us was drunker.

After he fucked me, we slept apart in the big bed with a mattress too soft for my back. Sometime beyond the middle of the night, about four, I woke to the sound of the ghost train churning past with garbage and mail from the other end of the city. I heard the cars slow on their tracks and, near me, the even breathing of this man I'd never see again.

1991

There were already these rumors then about gay cancer, and some people saying it could be worse. This would be my last night of taking chances.

※

Rich and I were sitting outside at the Fox and Hounds one evening that autumn, the first year. He was telling me something of no particular import, staring at the couple at the next table as though addressing them, while I toyed with my clam chowder, watching the spoon make dents in the thick white glop, playing at how many little mushroom and clam bits I could capture on the silver edge. I glanced at him. In a heartbeat and for the hundredth time I picked up on the exact shape of his eyes, round as coins from the bridge of his nose almost to the outer edge, where they taper into almond ends. And the color, nearly hazel when the sun hits them directly, in shadow more like copper.

I asked him to come over for the night. I let myself in first and called out for Henry, who of course was probably at Gary's. That was one of the strangest things that happened that year: as Rich and I got closer, so did Henry and Gary. They slipped from pity to love almost imperceptibly, and to this day I don't exactly know what kind of lovers they were, under the circumstances. Before he was sick, Gary'd had a chance with Henry and blown it, treating him badly. Now Henry became his best friend, his greatest admirer, his father and mother and brother all in one. Gary became Henry's avocation.

Rich got us two beers from the kitchen while I neatened the bedroom, shoving magazines into drawers and dumping dirty clothes in the closet. We picked up the conversation from the bar again. I could almost believe as I listened to him go on about the people he worked with—the fussy loan officer at the IMF and the long-suffering technical editor who wanted to go back to school and the receptionist who had one personal crisis after another and the accounts receivable clerk who refused to have a sonogram but instead went to a psychic to find out if her child was a boy or girl—I could almost believe that only this mattered, just sitting on the sofa with the last man I had ever expected to love so near me I could smell his scent, familiar from the first. I

1991

could almost believe it, and then we fell into a heavy-flannel silence, and I knew we were about to go to my room and make love, and I debated whether to ask him to put on some music he liked so we could prolong the moment or whether I should just go ahead. I tried to think clearly: Was this really what I wanted? Would it turn out all right? I could almost believe that I deserved to be this happy, in such an ordinary moment.

I'm alone too much. I hear them say this on the messages they leave, and sometimes when I pick up the phone they tell me themselves. I am much too alone. I am too much alone. But I have not given in. I go to work when I can. I run my errands when I want to. I see my doctors. I don't hide, much, any more than I used to. Any more than I have to.

"Wake up, boy!"

"Calling you again, where are you?"

"Man, what is with you?"

I eat, but I can't keep my weight up. I know this virus is killing me, but in fact I am briefly beautiful. My eyes are actually getting lighter. I think sometimes they will turn into mirrors, and then people won't be able to look me in the eye anymore, because they'll only see their own faces, convex, the way they look in supermarket mirrors meant to prevent crime.

I just reach the bank before it closes. The man behind me in line for the safety deposit vault mumbles to himself as he goes through a stack of papers with a heavy rubber band around them. The clerk who hands me a form to fill out has a cross of ashes on her forehead. Passover and Easter, so soon.

The teller says nothing when I bring back my completed card. She merely adds it to her stack, clacking it smartly against the pink granite counter that is older than both of us. She takes down her set of keys and leads me into the vault. At my box she puts her key in the top lock and waits for me to insert mine. Our arms almost touch as I take the box down.

"Do you want a room?" I nod my head and she leads me to a cell, flips on the bare bulb, shows me the button to push when I'm ready to come out, shuts the door, and locks me in.

1991

Before my mother died the only item in this box was my birth certificate. Now my bronze baby shoes are here, and Mom's plain gold band, her father's fob, a copy of her uncontested will. It is strange to see these solid objects beside the stapled sheaf describing in abstract but exacting terms the items she owned and who should have them. It is the will I came for, but I slip her ring onto my pinkie. It never left her hand until the hospital cut it off during her first stay. My father had it resoldered, as a surprise, but though he presented it to her on their anniversary, she never left the hospital to wear it. The hand this empty circle belongs on is gone to mold, washed in one direction, one final time, and buried in plain earth according to custom and law. I prefer to burn. And leave the rings on my fingers.

I wonder if it was like this for Mom, when she inherited her father's watch. No boy for her father to leave it to, and of course she never wore it herself. Her father's lifetime of vest buttons marred the gold finish. Inside the case skates a tiny enameled drama of moon and stars and clouds, behind the numbered hours. I wind the stem and hold the ticking to my ear. I will lock it in the dark again when I go, and it will tick out its measured little grains to the walls of a metal box. Maybe I will come to wind it every day and lock it up again promptly. A kind of penance for enduring. Why shouldn't I? It is never too early to become a madman. I'll learn from it. There is a sharp knock at the door.

"Through?" asks the woman. "We're about to lock up." I push the steel box back into its empty slot in the wall. After I am in daylight again, I remember I am wearing Mom's ring, snug on my pinkie.

A fine drizzle is falling, droplets clinging wherever they can, on the tree branches clotted with nubbins too young even to be buds. My mother's voice reassures me as I tuck my scarf closer: *The flowers need a drink.* The drowsy soreness in my joints tells me to go home, climb into bed, and prepare: My system is on alert against some new intruder. But I survived winter.

It's Friday. Erev Shabbat. I've called in sick to work again. There's nothing to prevent me from resuming all but the most stressful tasks. I couldn't face work yesterday or today. Malaise they call it. My mother's voice warns me: *We have to save our sick days for when we need them.* Maybe I need them now.

1991

Two old men I haven't seen since I moved to this street guard the parking lot by the liquor store. One of them is cultivating a muddy patch with tiny evergreens, packing soil around the new roots, swaddling the mounds in burlap against another cold snap, weighing the trees to the ground with bricks as if they might run away. The old man raises a hand at me. I raise mine too. Starlings scramble between the holes left empty for more saplings, fighting over the dried bread scattered among bottle caps and broken glass. When their bread falls in, they hop in after to retrieve it and flap their wings a few times to get back out, never bothering to fly.

I know where I am going.

They're finally breaking ground for something new on the lot near the house I shared with Rich. Off and on these past few weeks, I've watched the workmen clear the trees and carve a square depression into the earth. Whatever is planned, it won't be another house. Probably more condos, just as I predicted, with generous underground parking. I lace my fingers through the fencing around the site and peer down, bellying over the pit, pressing diamond shapes into my skin. It has begun to rain harder, soaking my hair and shirt.

When the Hindus lay the foundation for a house or town, they follow a checkerboard pattern with places for every deity. Each corner goes to a demon goddess, and the center is preserved for solemn Brahma, to prevent squabbles. I'm beginning to think I should have made corners for Rich and me when I redesigned our house, that I should have laid a mandala under my plan, put the center of the house in the hands of some domestic deity.

"Hey!" A workman with his hard hat off waves to get my attention. "Get back! That's not safe!"

I thought I could open the dark heart of that old house and simply borrow light from outside. But I miscalculated. A seam opened, and the cold was unbearable.

My friends' problems are all the same. Their lovers—some of whose names I haven't bothered to learn, because how long will they be in the picture anyway?—repeat the same small range of indignities. One is giving mixed signals, one can't commit, one wants too much. Their

1991

bosses, like mine, are opaque creatures whose motivations one is always scrambling to decode, whose occasional acts of kindness can be read more than one way, perhaps as sabotage attempts meant to keep one on one's knees long after gratitude fades. Their families are suffering disease or alcoholism or psychic pain of one stripe or another.

How long have I been performing for all of them anyway? Nodding my head, doling out possible solutions. It occurs to me that I haven't always felt I had to be *on*, had to be with it, to be of value to my friends. Wasn't there a time when I only had to be present? Think back. I can't remember ever finding friendship simple. It always seemed to harbor potential hazards if the barter it was based on didn't go well. Oddly, the simplest friendship I can recall is one that got hopelessly complicated: my first love, with my junior high and high school friend Tom Braivier. But that friendship had a before and after stage. Before: how easy it was to simply be with him, day after day through the long days of summer, evening after evening doing homework or bicycling our quiet block after dinner. After: he reached for me carelessly and unexpectedly in his car one night. We'd just dropped off our dates and sat alone drinking beer behind the 7-Eleven. After that exchange a furtive, homeless feeling floated between us, a need that knew its name and shamed us. The barter was real. It felt unavoidable until it was complete, each time. There was only the barter after a while. Tom was less sad than I was to say goodbye after graduation. But I don't think he could have been more relieved than I was.

Maybe now just being present is the performance for me, because in fact I'm always somewhere else, a not-pleasant place most of the time, a place I would go with a friend if I could. But that I can't wish on the people I still, with reluctance, remember to love.

I'll take a walk through Rock Creek Park. That will make something I can chat with the friends about. I saw a heron there one day, on an overflow from a dam I didn't know existed. The bird held itself so still, I thought at first it was a decoy. When I crept up to get a better look at it, it turned its head neatly to look back at me. Then it turned away again. As if it had been there all this time without me and wouldn't move again after I was gone.

1991

"David, I'm getting worried about you."

"David, sorry to call you at home, hope you're feeling well. I was hoping to find you there. Call us back, today if you can."

I have to hang on to that job. That's one of the things I bet friends would tell me, if I ever called them back.

I'm looking for the cemetery in Rock Creek, making my way toward a little path I know off 27th Street. The sun is out again, the pavement giving off an odor like the memory of itself as fresh cement. The rain has washed all variation from the overcast sky above the rooftops, bringing blossoms and branches to the ground. Here and there are wet, horned prints where a dead leaf has fallen and been washed away. In an alley, the headlights of an empty black Cadillac halo in the damp.

When the ground sinks under my feet, like newly turned sod, I know I'm close to the path. I almost slip but right myself against a broken headstone that leans like an old tooth against others in the bushes. At the top of the hill is a small park, with the cemetery fenced off from it by formal black gates. I've come the back way, to spend time with the dead—black families who sleep outside the gates. From here I can see the cozy back entrance of a Woodley Park apartment building, near a street sign that says 27th and Mill. I've never tried to find a way into the official cemetery, with its neatly kept graves and circumspect paths for the living. The iron gates are irredeemably locked.

The park's unprotected graves seem dug at random, most of them in such bad shape you can't read the inscriptions. Except for a big black obelisk set off by a chain near the center of the site. The family name, Harrold, is carved on the stone in plain Roman lettering. That's what I would like, if my family will allow it and if I decide not to be cremated. To hell with it. I'll be buried at sea or donated to science. They will either never find me or know everything about me.

The Harrold family slab is crumbled at one corner, exposing a chasm. When I step closer to look, my feet sink an inch into mud. Who could stand to live in this perfectly respectable apartment building, knowing what's here? There's a gas grill a few yards away, lawn furniture, and a couple of chaise longues for sunbathers. I back carefully off the unstable plot, threading my way back to the path I'd come along,

1991

skidding on another soft spot in the earth, recovering my footing, and picking my way uneasily past the first clump of graves. I should come back again, until I'm comfortable there. I should look into living at 27th and Mill, so I can barbecue or sunbathe in this place of the dead, since I belong as much as anybody, inside or outside the gates.

※

Indian summer visits. It's cool in the shade, but when I walk into full sun my hair feels metallic. I struggle not to squint. Under trees I settle down to watch the kids play. Lunchtime in the park is all I like about my job now. Maybe it's time to quit. My lunch bag crackles in the ozone-tinged air. All around me bob the heads of straight and curl, dark and light and one red, and all those little brains having new ideas, all those little synapses firing fresh and elastic and sharp, thinking all the old things in new ways.

Meg says gently almost every day that I've missed something on a bid or lost an important piece of information. I have explanations. We know what is really happening. In my head something is building—a pressure, a kind of heavy unreality that makes me take the wrong things calmly. The things that matter. But then I'll snap over the stupid things. Always, all of it, calm or not, with a bitter taste in my mouth, as if the ddI in its magnesium buffer has dissolved on my tongue instead of a pinch of it going down to do me good.

This afternoon it's a relief to get into the subterranean, ivy-smelling cool of the Metro. On the escalator I crane my neck back like a kid, watching the pale ribs of the curved tunnel move over me, immaculate except for a few ghostly water marks. The train threads itself through the dark eye of the tunnel and halts at the platform. The doors slip open and closed. One man tries to board after the second warning, and the doors clamp down once, twice, and finally release his brown attaché case. He stands with his feet apart on the crowded train, a little bewildered maybe at the sudden orange interior and the change in temperature. His upper lip sweats lightly, and he clears his throat, checks his case for damage.

The train pulls out of the station and straightens so the windows at

1991

the ends of the cars line up and seem like endless reflections of the one we're in. But it's all different people, sitting where we ought to sit, standing where we thought we were.

They're rebuilding one of the escalators at the Woodley Park Metro, encased it in plywood. I can see over the top as I walk up the other escalator, its denuded steel frame like the empty track of a shut-down roller coaster, the conveyor mechanism stilled.

I walk the four blocks to the Arms. Everybody is gone. I peer in through the glass doors. Across the empty lobby, the elevator doors and the door to the back staircase have been removed, so I can see they've started to gut the place already, though it still doesn't show from the outside. I wonder when and whether I'll see the project finished. I come away from the doors and startle a brace of sparrows scattering themselves in the dusty planters at the entrance. It's hotter today than it has been. Where was I headed? Where was it I thought was so important?

There's a woman walking toward me on the street, in a smart black suit, carrying a briefcase. I know her. "Marcia! What a surprise."

"I'm sorry?"

"Marcia. Marcia. Right? David Baum? This is your building, right? Mine, too."

The woman looks up at the Courtland Arms. "This building?"

"Is anything wrong?" I ask her. "I was passing by. I come by here once in a while."

"Are you lost?" she says.

Why did I think she was Marcia? Because this is where we often met? Does she look like Marcia at all? I can't get at the information about resemblance in this heat, it's locked away. "No. I'm not lost," I say. "You looked like someone."

The woman moves beyond me. The shadow passing over my face now is just my hand.

I always believed it was all in there—memories, stray phrases, facts and beliefs and lies you've told. Whatever you wanted or needed to remember, you could. Now I'm not sure that the mind doesn't begin to jettison at some point, throwing the ballast overboard. Only in my case, the ballast isn't enough apparently, and the crew is pitching the

140

1991

heavy and expensive stuff over as well. I keep finding myself several blocks from where I last remember being, and like a drunk I persist, clutching the remnant of the last memory until I can tack it to the next sure thing.

The air is moist and charged, another storm blowing in from the west, stirring the leaves fitfully on their stems and sending a loosened stop sign twisting like a weathercock. Is it another hundred-year storm?

I am on Columbia. This way is Belmont. To the left is 18th Street. 18th to T. T to 14th. I am on streets I remember. I am on streets I remember. At 14th the bus stops for me alone, and the driver who lets me board has something wrong with one eye. Rheumy and red-rimmed. The other is a clear hazel that seems to see through me. His round head is fuzzed with a gray Afro, close-cropped, and his mouth presses into a generous frown each time he turns the heavy steering wheel.

He tells the woman, "He's had a series of complications. He just took another turn for the worse."

"How many in your family?" she asks.

"Three. We all have children of our own." He brakes too fast. "My mother passed in 1980, and he didn't expect to live this long." The woman hums a little, and I ring for my stop.

At home, I fight it, but I have to lie down. Traffic below, an intermittent white noise, and the afternoon sky. Already like twilight, the blue of a pigeon's back. One curious wisp, not like a cloud, not like anything, seems not to move. There are no planes in sight, and anyway it is vertical, but otherwise it could be jet stream. Close to Venus, the evening star. Somewhere else in my mind I am back on my parents' wide patio, the sky then this shade of blue now. The brush of white floats just above the high branches of trees across the street, at the bottom edge of my window. It won't be snagged. Troubling, unexplained, it floats.

※

I call into the office to say I'll be there at noon. When I get there, a note from Meg on my desk says, *See me*. I go to her office. She asks me to close the door. The whistling in my ears tells me the blood has drained from my face into my extremities. I am ready to run. My

1991

fingertips tingle. My muscles contract from the belly out: chest tight, shoulders up. I feel a stone in my throat. She begins.

This time it's a meeting I've missed. Her eyes are sympathetic, head tilted. All she is saying is that she told the client I was double-booked and sent someone else to cover the meeting instead. But I know she is trying to tell me it's time.

She sent someone else. Instead. What Alice does now, every day, perhaps I could have done. In another version of my life. The stone comes unlodged just so I can talk through it sideways, rushing out the garbled words.

"Meg, I . . . I've been trying to make good on every promise I make, and I think I deliver what I've promised, but I can't promise things I can't do, or control—"

She steps back as if I've pushed her. But she sounds calm when she speaks. It isn't that I don't deliver, she tells me, it is that I am losing . . . ground. That is how she says it. I am losing ground. She says she is sorry.

Sometimes the most unlikely people have everything to say about your life. You go along expecting anything but this: that you'll stand before a man or woman whom you considered a friend but who in fact has little or no context for your life, nor you for theirs, and they will deliver you such a blow—

"David, I admire what you're trying to do but . . ."

They will deliver you a mortal blow without half knowing, and that will be that. The power to change your life fundamentally.

"I'm afraid we have to ask you to resign. I'm sorry."

Maybe she is sorry. Maybe she does have to ask. But she isn't afraid. I am. I slide my fingers along the edge of her desk without once dropping my eyes, because I know just where the edge is, my fingertips have pressed it often while she considered my work for years. For almost six years. For six years just shy a few months. It sounds like nothing. It was. If I had not been diagnosed the same year I got this job, I would have taken more chances, maybe, moved on, been someone's partner. But I thought I had security here. All I had to do was stay on. I will myself to look into and through her eyes.

1991

"I hope you know what you are doing, Meg."

"Unfortunately what I am doing is an act of survival. I cannot carry you on even a partial salary. I am losing business. I won't say that is because of you. Listen to me, David. You will get full disability benefits, sometimes consulting assignments. I'll talk you up to others. We won't let you fall through the cracks."

But if the cracks get any bigger, I'll have to fall. And you'll let go, all of you still classified as living, because if you don't let go I will take you with me. And by God I wish I could. I wish I could.

I leave her office and close the door as softly as if a sick person sleeps behind it. I walk to the office I shared with Alice. She doesn't pretend not to know. The other staff were standing strangely silent in the corridor and disappeared into their offices as soon as I came downstairs.

"David. David. This was not the way to do this." Alice puts out her hand like I am about to fall. I comfort her. Does she mean there is a way to do this?

"It's okay. It's okay." I retrieve my briefcase, turn off my work lamp, walk a few steps down the hall, keep walking, until I am on the street. I have missed several moments in the trip. I am on the street, still walking, and the bus is pulling up to the curb, as if on cue. I board. I cannot find a seat so I stand.

I want

The bus is very hot and a child is crying.

I want

I have begun to sweat where my collar meets my Adam's apple and beneath my arms.

I want

Also I am sickening. I have grown so accustomed to a baseline constant queasiness, a feeling that something is building onto itself inside me like a fungus, that I no longer remember when I didn't feel this way.

I want

to scream. I want to scream.

And in my mind I do scream. I scream as I haven't since I was a boy or rather since I was a teenager coasting downward faster than I

1991

wanted to on a ride that was supposed to be fun, that was billed to me and represented to me and sold to me as fun. The stone in my throat has become molten and I feel it sliding wrong-way hot and liquid down my windpipe I could cough but don't instead I scream harsher more acrid until I taste the bitterness of bile and the salt of phlegm until I see bright white hot dots spinning past my eyes in mandalas parabolas I scream until my own ears hurt, until the inside of my throat feels like sandpaper burlap unwashed linen corkboard I scream a scream that is fingernails down a blackboard that is tires squealing against pavement that is an alarm in traffic that is a smoke detector gone off that is an air raid siren that is a woman tackled from behind on a dark street that is a young man whose young lover is taken from him suddenly that is a child cheated out of the swing on the playground that is children tormenting the one child that's different that is children begging the two boys circling to *get him get him gethimgethimgethim.* I scream until I can't scream more then I scream more until I imagine I am being begged to stop and until I imagine I am begging to be allowed to stop I scream until I am not—

"—Enough!"

Voices in the hall, first one woman's, then another's. They are laughing.

"I can't get Jim to go. I couldn't *drag* him to one of those things."

"Oh, I know. Mine's the same way. All right then, see you tomorrow."

"All right."

Light squeaking steps on a polished floor somewhere recede. The lower of the two voices says, "I give those two a year, tops."

A reddish light beyond my lids. Something bright, just above me. A terrible thirst. A terrible, terrible headache. Again. Cold in the bones. I have a bone in my throat.

What I remember is not the panic but the shame afterward. They stopped the bus for me. Someone fanned me, and I sat right on the dirty sidewalk. These strangers stayed with me until the paramedics came.

"Morning, Mr. Baum. Well, if you'll just roll on your side I'll help you ascend the throne here."

1991

Outside a siren wails to silence. I remember being inside that dying sound myself. I was brought here.

"Someone new is getting help," I tell the medical attendant.

"Mmm-hmm. Okay, here's this. You can wipe. Go ahead."

"My head."

"What's that?"

"My head hurts."

"Would you like more painkiller?"

"I think so."

"Okay. I'll put a note here, we'll see if we can fix you up."

I lie for a long time alone. The light changes. At first the patterns from the blinds rested on my left leg. Now they have stretched to my right. Was I always awake? I can't look at my legs, can't look at anything for long, because in addition to the headache I have a nausea that is worse when I try to focus. I don't like to close my eyes, though, because then I feel as if I'm drunk and the invisible room is whirling around me. A technician brings a rattling tower of trays to my door, depositing one in front of me. Right behind her is a nurse in a fuzzy purple sweater I can't look at for long. Her face is familiar.

"You're sitting up, that's excellent. You must be feeling better."

I know they are paid to be upbeat, but really. "I feel terrible," I remind her.

"We can probably step up your meds today, and that should help," says the nurse, who says her name is Belinda. Nurses and techs have first names and doctors have last names. "We had to keep them low because we really didn't know what might be happening with you."

"What day is it?"

"Wednesday. You've been talking to us and things the last few days, do you remember?"

I try to shake my head.

"Well. That's not too surprising. You've had a trauma. You were in intensive care for a few days, and then when you seemed to be more conscious we got you in your own room. Your friend has been visiting every evening around this time, so now you'll get to talk with him. He'll fill you in."

1991

"What's wrong with me?"

"Well, a couple of things happened at once. You're here because you had a seizure. But Dr. Millidad is on rounds tonight. It's probably better if he goes into all the detail."

She gives my hand a brief squeeze. Her fingers are icy, or I am boiling hot. Either way it feels good. A disregarded car alarm goes off on the street. It plays out the patterns it knows, one after another, for a long time. It doesn't wind down. It just stops.

1992

I still belong to the world, even as I watch my bones emerging steadily from the melting fat, as my face hollows and my eyes pale and my mouth swells and still I burn at night like a stove with its pilot light always lit, warming no nourishment, and everything I eat goes through a fierce wringer inside me and rushes out of my bowels in a wrecked stream. Still I turn my pencil against the pad methodically when I sketch, just simple shapes to keep in practice, rotating to keep the graphite point even. I cannot relinquish all I know of myself: still I talk, move, have loves and hatreds and grudges born of both, crave a movie, seek the cool side of the pillow, prefer white chocolate to dark chocolate, dark to milk, lie to my family and friends, remember how I hated the way Rich folded my shirts, once dreamed of being a pilot or a mathematician, and before then thought I'd be king. I want birthday cake at least five or six times a year, am just as happy with the beer Henry calls piss as with something expensive, am sorry I never saw a funnel cloud touch ground or traveled to Canada to see the geese return north, and wish that I'd already found some way to tell my father, maybe that morning in the garage when I was seventeen, that I love men.

By midnight every night, in addition to the quickening tick of thoughts, my temperature creeps upward until it's really no longer a matter of whether I'm asleep or not. I've in any case begun to dream. I doze lightly sometimes around two, in the suffocating shell of my body, mixing into my sleep images of cooking lobsters of mummies of being buried alive of walls closing in of blankets tangling, and I often wake up briefly, struggling with the feeling of pulling my head through a tough layer of latex, of seeking with every muscle the open neck of a sweater made of asphalt, every muscle straining and the dog rapping at

1992

the door downstairs with a paw that is a mallet is a photograph is a body thumping at the door is—

The newspaper hitting the front door at six-thirty in the morning has come to be my favorite sound. I hear the delivery man drop one at almost every door of the hollowed square of the third floor. When I hear him, the night is over. There might have been a time when this was a dreadful sound, dragging me out of bed and into the world. Now that sleeping is harder work than being at work ever was, I look forward to the moment I hear the *Post* drop. Between that and the ringing of the alarm an hour later I have my deepest sleep, as though the newspaper man has delivered me and given me permission at last to relax.

❋

Lerner is looking over the lab results that show us why I am getting purple bruises again. One of my blood-clotting factors is low. "This is not good. I think it might be the gancyclovir."

"I don't want to take it anymore. Can I stop?"

"You might just have to start again, or start on something else."

"My vision is still 20/20."

"It isn't just the vision."

"What about taking this thing out?" I lift my shirt away to indicate the ugly plastic catheter.

Lerner is still looking over my blood work, muttering to himself as if I am not even here. "Well. That's not good either."

"Could I get it back in later? If I need it? It makes me feel like a freak."

"Nobody knows it's there. And I don't think we have decided to take you off the gan—"

"I know it's there."

Lerner moves the stacked folders around on the side table, as if by shuffling them he could pick me out a new medical history. "It's not necessary to take it out, even if we have to suspend the gancyclovir."

"Not necessary from a medical point of view."

"From a medical point of view it may even be detrimental. Every surgery introduces a new opportunity for infection. I would like you to stay on the gancyclovir while we try to clear up this other problem some other way."

"And add another medication to the regimen? No thanks."

"David. You may not want to hear this, but we aren't really at a stage now where some of these treatments are optional."

"Everything is always optional."

The catheter stays in.

Jodie calls to tell me something funny. Gina was doing something Jodie didn't like. Jodie told her to stop.

"I'll stop tomorrow," said Gina.

"No," said Jodie. "Today. This is the last day."

"Uh-uh," said Gina. "After today there are more days forever."

A freakish warmth settles in, but not spring. I try to take a walk every afternoon, two blocks square, my only trip out most days. I shuffle along like a pensioner, smiling mildly at the vendors, inhaling their coconut oil and candle wax, their vanilla incense and myrrh. Otherwise I like to sit by the window in my blue room, listening to the cassette tapes Henry used to make for our parties. *I know you'll miss me.*

Rich has taken to making sudden appearances at my apartment door, ringing up and standing in my living room with groceries and jars of homemade soup or tomato sauce. "I had extra," he explains. He'll lean over to kiss me, before I have even invited him to. I turn my head so he can kiss my cheek. I could pick up any harmless thing now, and it would all be over. Too bad if I hurt his feelings. I have to protect myself.

I dream myself at the rink again, another winter day. It's such an ordinary dream, obeying the rules of reality. I am bundled up tight, watching my friends skate by on the Reflecting Pool. I have discovered that I can look directly at the sun for several seconds if I peek at it with my bad eye while winking my left. Only the faintest halo in a red sky. Wave at Rich as he goes by with his mittened hand aloft. My closest friends put up with me. Wave, wave.

At the end of your life there is so much time. It's lumpy and uneven, badly blended, but it's all around you, moving through you. Wasting. In the dream I just sit there. In my life now, it's the same.

The girl in the pink leotard is there, wearing blue. I wave at her, and though her feet still understand the ice, the rest of her body pulls her off balance. Poor girl. In only a few minutes she'll be too old.

Rich swings past again, waving. I nod so he knows I see. But he knows. He wants to make sure he sees me.

Always looking back over your shoulder, thinking: There I was happy, and work was as light as a game, but I didn't yet realize. For years it lasted, this relief that life was so much easier than school. Life's daily rules were comprehensible and flexed like the rubber seats of the swings we played on as children, flying us upward, bringing us down, simple as gravity.

When you get as sick as I am getting, you have to be careful which version of the truth you are telling to whom and for what outcome. It is no mean feat to spend the better part of a week chasing all over town and making phone calls to people you'd almost rather die than request a favor from (my old boss, for example, or Lerner, whose care I haven't been able to afford for months), just so you can document a disability claim. Then to fill out the paperwork and wait to undergo the screen-

1992

ing that determines whether you are pathetic enough for the assistance. Meanwhile, one morning you have to see a prospective client your old boss has gone to some trouble to throw your way. You shower, shave carefully around the most recent rash, apply Bacitracin and coverstick to the bloody places, hunt for a pair of slacks that will stay up, then for a suit jacket to go with the only slacks that fit, struggle to match two dark socks, check carefully against the written list of items for your briefcase because your short-term memory is not what it was, and get yourself out the door on time for an interview with the potential client. You can tell that he can tell, before you've been in the conference room ten minutes. He isn't just sizing up your résumé and portfolio. He is assessing whether you will finish the job.

You come home running another fever, catch a couple of hours of dream-fractured sleep, wake up, and look in the refrigerator for something, anything, that you might want for dinner. Your friends bring you food now without even pretending as they used to that they made too much lasagna by accident, or casserole, or soup.

Sometimes you are so hungry you have to remind yourself that if you eat anything rich or hard to digest—basically anything you really want—you will pay later. Sometimes you give in to the craving anyway: for ice cream, for a big bowl of Green Giant peas in a butter sauce with slivered almonds, or an order of fried chicken. The worst is when you go to the trouble of getting something you've longed for, then take a single bite and can't stand it anymore. Within minutes the very smell of whatever you once wanted sends you pitching to the toilet. You rinse your mouth and wipe your lips and drink a Coke and take one each, again, of whatever medication you just disgorged, costing yourself a hundred after insurance in just one sick instant. You know you should call your father back, because he has left three messages for you in a week. You should call your sister, who has left you only one but probably wanted to call you more often. You flip channels on the TV instead, hardly watching, not even bothering to turn any lights on as another day ends. You will lose your apartment if the city doesn't come through soon.

What makes up *now* to you has assorted names already. You understand—again—that comprehending the basic daily colors, the grays and reds of depression and panic, is no protection from being surprised by them—again, each time, and at the same time.

In the dream you understand that depression is a square and panic a triangle on its nose. The warmth and heft of your friends, back from the ice to collect you and take you home, is a circle.

You should be—are—surprised to be alive. Grateful. What suffering, really, at this point, can you indicate? Not what you expected. Not at all what you expected.

In the dream, one thing is different. When you stand, there is no difficulty. It's the way it used to be.

Your life is not well blended now, that's all.

I step over dead Christmas trees shrouded in plastic at the curbs. Tinsel glitters everywhere in the brittle streetlight: scattered in the trodden grass, ground into the icy mud, glinting in the living trees where birds have woven it into their nests. It is funneled up into the wind, then swept into the gutter, where it slips beneath the streets, floating on the slow current of storm sludge, down through the sewers to the edge of the city. Months from now people will find some of it above ground, clinging to their carpets, tucked into their sock drawers. Tinsel gets into everything.

Sparkling, glowing, gleaming, bitch-cold winter. The leftover Christmas lights are mostly white stars, a few inert strings on dying trees at curbside, little clusters in wreaths still on doors, outlining awnings and gutters and walks, weighing into the darkness of bushes. Leaning into the promise of the windows that are golden, ochre, lemon, russet, silver. From a single bulb behind drawn curtains in a darkened room, or flickering with the celebratory candlelight of strangers, or fizzing blue from the shifting programs on TV. Mine is among the unlit windows.

At our old house, Rich once waited for me to come home, his face like a boy's pasted nose-first to the window, above a loosened shirt and necktie. When he opened the door to me, the warmth from inside enfolded us.

"Hey." He opened his arms. "Hey. Come here."

We stood there like that for a minute on the darkened porch. He took my hang-up bag. "Come inside," he said. "It's cold out." He shut the door behind us, sealing in the warmth and light.

1992

Tonight there's a dull, lopsided moon, nearly full, with a thin slice clipped from its left side and a surface the acrid white of aspirin, so matte and bright you can't make out pocks or shadows you know are there. By midnight the moon hangs low among the still, sickly trees in the street. In the wee hours it hovers over the alleyway between the tops of two low buildings.

Mornings are worst. Choose between lying here with a pillow over your face, hiding from the light that reddens your field of vision in the bad eye, and going to the kitchen to fix your own damn tea. No one comes to help.

The teakettle whistles. Get up slowly or you'll get dizzy. Take the kettle off finally, pour the water into a dirty cup you found by the sink. Add a fresh bag. Someday you will be dead, but not yet.

FEAR NOT.

I never once designed, nor ever will design, a building I would like to be remembered for. One that would be known as mine. To hell with it anyway. Most people walk into great buildings, or drive past them daily, without knowing or caring who designed them or who laid the bricks. Much less what keeps the walls up. For years people passed the garage James Hampton worked in, never suspecting the Throne of Heaven lay beyond its plain wooden doors.

※

In an overequipped lounge chair at the clinic, I wait to have my eyes checked again while Henry waits outside to take me home. I have switched medicine twice, and I am still losing vision in the left, my good, eye.

The RN is close by. "You feeling okay?"

"My head is hurting again."

"Lie back if you want. We'll have the doctor come in when he's ready. It might be a while anyway." She dims the light and leaves me.

At my first eye exam years ago, the ophthalmologist shone a light into my eye and told me to look away. And there against the white wall, the red orb of my retina's shadow loomed like Mars. Not a perfect circle. There are very few in nature.

"Clear," she had said. "No bright patches. That's good."

1992

In the near dark now I begin drawing basic shapes behind my eyelids. The triangle. The circle. The square. I draw them in silver, then gold. I make them cutouts from construction paper in blue and pink and red, because that's how I remember them. I arrange five slim triangles around a circle in a star shape. It is soothing but sad.

The square is overrated. The triangle is much more economical, and every bit as stable unless you turn it on point. The circle, of course, was the beginning of geometry: measuring the earth. I attempt the hyperbolic paraboloid, a series of curves made with adjacent straight lines to form something like a large ruffle, with an arc below and an arc above. It creates a remarkably stable, if ugly, roof for large buildings. I go back to simple shapes.

When I come home, the building super flags me down on the way to the elevator. A gentleman called for you, he says, in his old-fruit voice. He hands me this pink triangle full of chocolate, with a red heart and a blue heart and a yellow heart on the top, with these long dark hearts at their feet—shadows. And the super says, oh and this too. And he hands me—what are those things called?—a sticky note with this scrawled, half-assed message:

David, sorry I missed you. Happy Valentine's Day. I want to see you tonight or sometime soon if you want to. Either way, enjoy these and know that you mean a lot to me. P.S.: I will be home by 6:00.

—Rich

Here he is as usual, giving me something I can't fucking have anymore. Twelve Chocolate Truffles Net Weight 8 oz (225g). In a pink triangular box with three scrawled hearts pinning down shadows. I raise the lid. Truffles smelling of alcohol, shaped like half ellipses with nipples. I am not supposed to have these, and he should know that.

Two at the apex, four in the middle, and six on the bottom. Tucked in open gold sarcophagi, each one. He is trying to kill me.

Sorry I missed you. That's a joke, right? He isn't and he doesn't. He can't. I was the one calling him last month, twice with no answer.

I want to see you tonight if you want to. There is a double meaning here. I want to see you if you want to. There are too many verbs and too many I's and you's. I can't make it out, but there is a joke in there somewhere.

1992

Enjoy these and know that you mean a lot to me. Why is he putting all these verbs in? He is trying to get something past me. I can't eat these and he gives them to me just to make a fool of me.

I will be home by 6:00.

Now I have all this chocolate on my lap that I can't keep in the house. I will give it to the super and keep the box for myself. I measure its sides with my hands. About 14 by 10 by 10. I press the points of the base between my palms. The clock by my bed says six-ten, but I am not going anywhere.

❋

Henry says, "What is with you, anyway? What is with you?"

We have met for lunch in the soggy park near my old office. The flu season is past, the season of pollen begins. God knows what I have said this time. It can be the smallest thing, and these friends get so upset. How can I explain that this damp spring aggravates my impatience? Not with them, not with them, but with their thickness, their solid stupid will, their ideas about the way things are supposed to be. They want me to listen to their opinions. Worse, they want me to answer with mine.

But my friends don't like it when I say what I really think. They don't even know how much we all edit our thoughts before speaking. Until I got too tired to bother, I didn't know the extent of it. They continue to call and we make plans, which I appreciate. They tell me I look good and then get their feelings hurt when I say, *compared to what?* If my behavior is a hindrance, if my acid jokes and my insistence on the truth about my health are a problem for them—after all this time of telling me to tell them—well, I will certainly know by the silence of my telephone. Until then, I plan to behave exactly as I wish. I don't have time to be polite anymore.

Henry waits for an answer. What now? I ignore him. I don't even remember what I said. I wasn't even listening to him anyway. I watch the nannies watch the children. "If you scare the bee, you make him angry, then he stings you," explains one to an enraged child, who already came to the playground with a broken arm and now apparently has been stung on the good one, which he pinches with the fingers of the broken hand. He is crying so hard, so silently, that his bright red face

1992

seems about to implode. Henry stops waiting for his answer. He throws his empty bag in the trash and walks away. I don't have time to be kind anymore.

Each time that you know you are getting really sick, you fight it first, even if you weren't fighting before. You take your meds the way you were supposed to all along. You make at-home dinner plans with a few trusted friends, rent videos, try to focus on simple pastimes. In the night you sweat and get sicker. When you're done with the fever, you freeze. You try those images they teach in your support group: armies of white corpuscles fighting like soldiers in the tight corridors that carry blood. But picturing this battle-blasted landscape only worsens your claustrophobia. You sit by the window of your unkempt apartment, afraid to go out because you can't see well to cross the street and you're afraid of catching something horrible from a dirty fork in a restaurant and the last time you went out you nearly lost control before you made it to the bathroom. Your floors are covered in clothing, your table ringed with old glasses, the sink full of dishes, the machine full of unreturned messages. You sit by the window and imagine each cell shedding poison like tight clothing. Anything you have foolishly depended on eventually betrays you: your bowels, bladder, hands, legs, eyes, memory. Your body wants to shed whatever causes this trouble, even itself.

I finally allow myself to be hospitalized again. At least this time it's no surprise; at least I know what it is for. Detached retina, curable by surgery. After the cure, I get pneumonia, submerging me for days in fever and oxygen dreams. When I am better I can't stop wondering how much it will cost. I will be here a minimum of ten more days. Still, the gratitude for care settles over me like a light blanket, and sometimes in spite of the hallway noise and the drone in my head, I can doze. Sometimes in spite of everything, I do have exactly what I need, for ten minutes or an afternoon: no pain, and the sweet leaden sleep of recovery.

Henry and Alice are the first visitors after the gauze is off, bearing apple cider and Scrabble. "To celebrate that you can read again," Henry says. "Now, I know you're not supposed to have this." He pulls a jug and three disposable cups out of a bright blue plastic Safeway bag.

1992

"I'm not supposed to have anything," I say. "Let's drink to deprivation. What's up with that bag?"

"This? It's for recycling plastic bottles. You've seen these."

"I don't think I have. What a pretty blue. What a waste of a pretty color."

"You want it?"

"What for?"

"I don't know. Things."

"No. It's just trash."

"Okay." He pulls out three shiny party hats. Alice smooths the bag into a small square for her purse. My throat plumps up. "I'm very fond of you," I say.

Alice pulls my tray-table to the bedside. "We are very fond of you too, David." Together she and Henry turn letters face down on the maroon box lid. Dr. Millidad taps on the door, doing rounds.

"We'll be discharging you tomorrow, if you're ready to go," she says.

"Am I ready to go?"

She nods and smiles. "We won't see you for a while, I trust."

"I trust."

After she goes, Henry squeezes my shoulder. Alice shakes the lid and extends it to me for first pick. I hold it close so I can see.

"L. For Lucky."

Henry picks his and shows me. "X. Too bad. Alice?"

"A for Alice. It doesn't get better than that."

"No, it doesn't."

※

Henry helps me choose clothing for my birthday party: a new white shirt, the bright blue bow tie Rich gave me, and fresh khaki slacks. We arrive at Alice's fashionably late, with late-blooming roses. In spite of her great care clearing the menu with me, she didn't bother to inform me about the guest list, an absolutely Proustian circle of friends and acquaintances. There must be thirty people in her living room, waiting to go up on the roof deck to enjoy my last evening on earth.

Rich is here; I kiss his cheek. Henry hangs back, perhaps because he sees me all the time, or perhaps he is as embarrassed by this pageant as

1992

I am. I guess it's been decided for me, that this year, this birthday, before it is too late, will be the big bash reserved for the turn of a decade. My old friends and lovers crowd in to demonstrate how glad they are I am alive and how little they expect me to be next year.

※

My eyes again. My legs and arms. Paralysis now. Dear God. The fingers of one hand, curling toward the palm unless I smooth them out with the other hand along the sheet. My skin and head. When will it be my heart?

Friends have the weather on them when they come to visit. They bring its scent on their clothes. They leave all kinds of other things with me, but they can't leave me that, that rain smell, crushed brown leaves, ozone. They bring me flowers out of season that eventually bow and fade in their vases: blood-red gladioli, white roses, sticky mums scattering petals like nervous bridesmaids, African daisies as vibrant as dye. Why won't they bring me something that lasts? Or nothing at all. It's hard to be sure of the season anymore because of all these fucking flowers, because we can have whatever we ask for now. It's perverse. Bring me candy. Fuck the prohibitions. If it has to be gone, I want it gone because I've eaten it. Or bring me air fern. It needs nothing but our breath to grow.

The longer I stay, the more creative my guilty friends get. They do bring me things that will last, long past me: big-picture books for children, my cassette player and tapes, a baseball hat, a Hawaiian lei. And they bring me things that won't last because I am going to eat them: smuggled Chinese food and yogurt, Milk Duds, candy cigarettes, candy corn.

"It must be Halloween," I say.

All the seasons here blend together like the years themselves. In the world, sometimes seasons stay, but mostly all they do is go. Our eyelids turn colors inside. I remember. Gold and ozone for fall, blue and ice for winter. White for spring. The whole spectrum. Velvet black with orange spots for summer.

No, it's the sadness, I mean, that makes me turn suddenly to look again in a display window, sure he was there. Bright shopping-red for late summer. But it was only me. Or a mannequin.

"He's in and out like this. We're going to go. If he wakes up, let him know we stopped by."

"I will."

Rich is here. I turn my head. I can just see his outline.

"What's wrong with my eyes?" I ask. He leans close and tells me to repeat. I feel his breath on the bridge of my nose and smell its tangy, familiar sweetness like good tea. I am not even sure I hear his voice or that this is actually happening.

Do you remember that first summer, darling? he asks. *We had such a good time that whole first summer.*

How long have you been here?

A while. I've just been telling you things, little thises and thats. I thought you were sleeping.

He is crying. I must look pretty bad.

※

Jiri says, "David?" Shouting at me as if I am old. "We'll see you tomorrow, okay? You take care." But it's too late for that.

I can't hear my friends coming or leaving, because the doors here are silent. I don't know when I am alone.

FEAR NOT.

When I sit up sometimes I hear tenor voices, a chorus bringing its song ever higher, speeding the pace until the resolution draws off abruptly with a whoosh. Tonight the sound seems to draw the room's light in with it, higher and higher, dimmer and slimmer, the sound and the light spiraling together like coils of DNA, upward through the ceiling. The next thing I'm aware of is a cold, bruised flatness on the left of my face. A wet acid smell. Nearby, a fluttering presence. *Pitpitpit.* Wing beats or little footsteps come toward me and go away. *Pitpitpit* like the sound of feet against a tile floor. I'm lying on a cold floor.

Pitpitpit. Like Gina's feet in the hallway. Calling, *Mommy, Uncle David threw up.*

Jodie and Mama are there, lifting me from the murk and perching

1992

me on the rim of the tub, strangely soft, as if stacked with towels. A cool rag laps at my face.

"Goodness," Mama says, not an ordinary expression for her. "Dear, you had quite a fall. You're going to have a lovely bruise tomorrow. Try not to move, you'll pull out the rest of your tubes. Where did you think you were going?"

It feels like someone is pressing nickels into the back of my hand, my arm, then my hip. I wouldn't say it hurts exactly.

"Nothing broken, at least. Good thing your head is so hard."

"I'm sorry." I can hear my mother bundling soiled linens, cleaning up as if no time has passed since she had a houseful of kids. "Mama, I'm sorry."

"Nothing to be sorry about, Mr. Baum. Let's just get you a clean bed." A plastic bag rustles as it goes into a hamper I'm sure is marked with warnings. When the nurse returns, she and the medical technician confer briefly on what to do. I am pulled out of my gown, put in fresh clothing, and tucked back into a bed with clean, stiff sheets.

"I'm still in the hospital."

"Mmm-hmm. No, don't lay back yet," says the nurse. "Stay on your side for now. Here, we'd better prop a couple more pillows under you so you can be more on your back. There. What else, dear?"

"Water?" Already I feel myself drifting, opening like a plant to the bright light they have turned me toward, but a taste like battery acid leaks down my throat.

"What, dear?" She leans her head in more, blotting out the light.

"Water, please."

"How about a little ice?"

"Is my mom here?"

"Would you like us to contact your family?"

"Where's Gina?"

"Who?"

"Tell her not to be scared."

"What, dear?"

"Tell Gina I'm okay."

"Now, here. Can you drink this, son?" I am handed a glass of water

1992

but can't make my hand close around it. She holds it for me, tipping it to my face, not spilling a drop.

Rich is by my bed again. He is asking me a question. *Do you remember that first summer?* I turn my head. I can see his silhouette from the waist to the neck. He asks me again, *Remember, darling? God, that was fun. God, that whole first summer.*

※

"David, my name is Dominga, how are you?"

"I'm in the hospital again."

"Yeah, I know. I'm a social worker here. We have some big steps to talk about."

"I have a will."

"Good. But that's not what I'm here for. I'm talking about getting you a good living situation when you leave the hospital. We need to get you some really good care at home. Or we need to find a place for you to be, pretty quickly."

"Are they discharging me?"

"They're thinking they will let you go on Friday."

"Am I that much better?"

"Not better enough to be on your own."

"They just need the bed."

"David, you have some options. Your family is in contact with me, and they are ready and happy to do what you want. I talked to your friend Henry. He really cares about you. He is working on getting you some care."

"How long have I been here?"

"Ten days on Friday."

"I see." Of course I don't see. They didn't even get to my eyes this time. The surgeon told me today even without the pneumonia, I'm no longer a good candidate. I didn't even know I was running.

※

Rich is by my bed again. Or is it Rich at all? Is someone there? Maybe I'm only remembering him. Maybe it's the same visit, his first.

1992

We are in a continuous loop, he and I. He is always here because he came that once. I will stay here because he wants to see me, and I will still be here after I am gone.

"They gave me the executive office," I tell him. "I'll be moving in tomorrow, if everything is ready."

"Which office?" Humoring me because he knows how much I enjoy telling it again.

"It's a triangular shape, with two glorious arched windows. You can see the Circle and Farragut Square."

"That sounds very nice," he says.

"Oh it is, it is. It's heaven."

❋

Cardboard, old furniture, foil, spent light bulbs. It is this that you came for, this that you will take home.

David, we need to know what your wishes are.

What does that mean?

Well. You have some options for care, and we need to know what you want.

I want all the care. I want all the options.

❋

The sadness, I mean. Like the one that you inhale deeply as you say, "It smells like sixth grade to me." That only happens at changes of season.

It seems to rain more then: The wind blows a different way, and you reorganize things in your pantry. You decide you wish to go play on the swings or jump in leaves or ice-skate after all these years. Even if it's still not quite time.

Those are my wishes. To line up the cans in the pantry and go play on the swings after all these years.

I hear my friends' voices and imagine them pulling their jackets on, impatient to pronounce our handiwork good before going along their way. Someone is getting a push, rocking their car out of ice. I hear them in the street. My house is surrounded by water.

1992

❋

It's the right time to skate.

❋

David. We could get you at-home care or, if you want, there happens to be a slot on the hospice floor; they don't come up quickly like that all the time. If you feel ready.

Where's my mom?

We called your father yesterday. He's on his way.

Is he scared?

Probably.

It's not a sadness. I give us all too much credit when I call it that. It's an extra smell or a shimmer in the light or a catch of the breath and a second glance into that window for someone who is gone, sure she is still there with your hand in hers.

It's somehow a certainty in the face of all the evidence that nothing ever changes.

Is that it? That nothing changes? After today there are more days forever?

❋

The catastrophe was so sudden, almost without warning. First, a low hiss and a cloud. Then the cave-in. Then silence. Then the wounded stirred beside the dead, and the death count mounted through the night and into the years. All from a moment as decisive as shutting off a single light.

60 seconds (") = 1 minute (')
60 minutes = 1 degree (°)
360 degrees = 1 circumference
A degree of the earth's surface = 69.16 miles at the equator.

The shapes came to me in the nicest colors this morning. The door of my house is bronze. I think I was still half dreaming, but I knew where I was. I am in the hospital. I don't know what day it is except that it can't be Friday, because I will be discharged on Friday. The triangles

1992

were pink and orange and blue and yellow and green and red. I made the red spin away, but it kept coming back, so I made it a game. Red is the panic triangle. Then the panic turned white and spun into the hot center of a star whose points were blue and yellow and green and pink and orange and red. When I saw it that way, with the colors arranged, I felt better about red coming back. The white center was cold and hot all at once, like ice. Like the center of the sun. The square was gone.

Mr. Baum. Want the bed up?

The room where we take coffee is silver.

The places I dream of always have some kind of breadth: sometimes it's a field, sometimes the lawns of my old neighborhood in Dallas, sometimes a desert. It is nice to sit up for a change, but nice goes away.

The more I allow it, the higher I go, fighting a giddy terror that this letting go can only free me higher, higher, until I'm so high I can't come down unbroken. I soar over the lawns or the poppies or the wheat or sand. The upturned faces of neighbors or strangers pivot to follow my easy arcs. I am not moving a muscle to do this; I'm physically as relaxed as a sleeper, which is in fact all that I am. I soar over a roof with copper shingles. The floors in that house are lead.

"Stay with me. Stay here." Rich is trying to wake me. He squeezes my hand and I squeeze back. I open my mouth.

"The stars at night, are big and bright."

"What, darling?"

"You're supposed to clap. One-two-three-four. Or say, boom-boom-boom-boom."

"Boom-boom-boom-boom."

"Deep in the heart of Texas. Reminds me of the one I love—"

"Boom-boom-boom-boom—"

"Deep in the heart of Texas."

Rich is laughing now. "You goof. Give me your hand."

I want to tell him that I'm awake. I know where I am. It's just that I can go to other places by thinking about them. I think he knows. He talks to me as if it's the same.

"Such a cold little hand." He covers it briefly with his. In the early days they would have made us wear latex. Now they know we don't catch our death so simply.

1992

Feel the shape of my hand in his. I thought that song about the stars was about a beloved's eyes. Imagine my hand with its fingers outstretched, white with blue veins and red pock marks. And the other hand I can't straighten, black and yellow bruises from the tubes. Such variegated, imperfect, heavenly bodies. Each a star dangling from a limb.

The people who love me bring weather, and time, and things they remember I love. They must get so bored.

※

Lift your arms and open them to a wide V, fingers taut and pointed, blood tingling down into your shoulder sockets like the little beads in a game you hold in your palm. Kick out of your shoes and rub your sore feet together. It has been such a long day. A sweet westerly breeze catches you up under the arms and buoys you an inch or so, then several feet, off the gravel-topped roof of your building.

It's been my birthday lately. All my friends are here, the whole map of Washington. But who is missing? I think a lot of people are missing.

※

Here is Rich. He sits beside me and simply rubs my head. My head is hurting so much more than it's supposed to. I feel hot. We must be outside somewhere. I want someone to take me inside please.

The Metro train bucks on the tracks underground, but we are cushioned from its friction. We can hear the rhythmic jolt of steel wheels across the joints of track segment, but we can't feel it. We sit and stand in the backmost car. A male voice announces each stop, pleasantly reminding us to take our personal belongings with us. Still we leave things behind, raining our carelessness on belongings personal and impersonal, as judiciously as the rain that pats the car's windows when we emerge above ground. Umbrellas, wallets, unfinished books, discarded newspapers, unmailed letters, eyeglasses, briefcases, gifts we'll never recover to give.

It takes them years to teach us to care about the things we are supposed to care about and to stop caring about the things that aren't supposed to matter. The problem is, the instructions were always in-

1992

complete. We are not supposed to walk on the grass, and even during an ice storm when the grass is dead, we are not supposed to complain that they have put down only a slender wire of sand for us to walk on. They told us not to laugh at the black kids who came to class on the bus, but they never told us what to do instead. We learned that silence is a safe bet. Turning away our faces, pretending not to notice someone was different was the only kind alternative.

My hand is a spade-shaped leaf, and the fingers are veins carrying sap to the webbed green tissue. I shake it, and the tissue dissolves, leaving five spindly points. My arm is a bare limb, and the bony points that were my thumb and fingers spread to make a perfect star.

A male voice announces each stop, pleasantly reminding us to take our personal belongings with us.

This is not my stop yet.

My first apartment in this city was on Columbia Road. I kissed him on our roof, a tiny cedar deck with built-in benches and iron furniture. One Fourth of July a neighbor climbed out to the forbidden part of that roof with his friends, where the air vents spun up from the gravel, and sat on the edge to watch the fireworks. He fell. I wasn't there. Once I poured champagne over the edge.

Dupont Circle. That's not my stop anymore. The 42 isn't my bus.

I went home with a guy who lived on Elliott Street, off Maryland Avenue, and stayed the rainy weekend. He slept in a loft there, with a skylight that showed a different day each morning and that leaked rain and ice onto our pillows. Union Station to the X8. The Sunday I left to go home, the bus never came, and I went to the station on foot. Back then the station was still slipcased in steel and looked like a munitions factory. As I turned the corner and approached the metal hulk the skies opened again, and by the time I reached the station I was soaked to the bone.

The city map contains four sets of the alphabet, excluding J, X, Y, and Z. There's an avenue for every state, but California has only a street. There are circles and squares, Federal Triangle and the Ellipse. The Capitol rotunda with a dome 180 feet high and 97 feet across. And beyond. There are bridges: Anacostia, Kutz, Case, and Roosevelt. Arlington Memorial. Key.

1992

There's the house where Rich and I lived on 16th Street. He grew two gardens there. We tried to rebuild from the inside out, but there was too much to the house we didn't know. Any S bus would take you there.

My first apartment without him had a lovely rooftop, on Columbia Road, but I couldn't afford it for long. I lived below 14th Street, at the U Street Metro station, almost the end of the alphabet, still unfinished, so I will never stop there. I used to take the bus.

This city is full of memorials.

My head is so heavy. It's like being in the pool in summer. Dunked, down to the grate, looking through the drain into a darkness beyond this unwatchable blue. I am dying, I think. I am dying, but I can open my eyes here. The chlorine sting is gone; I have breathed past the burn in my lungs. I am taking in water. I can see beyond the pool's painted bottom, past the aqua not found in nature, past the lost key chains and name tags, caught in the grate and waving past me. I can see in the dark. Simple shapes.

Deep cold. A pain where the breath comes from. A pain in my leg.

Where? Try to tell me. I will rub it. Can you show me?

I know you would do anything. Rub the life back in or out all the way if I could tell you where it is.

You don't have to tell me. I can try to find it.

I have to tell you.

I wish I knew what to say.

I don't like it when people know what to say. I want them to be idiots so I can hate them.

He is laughing. Why do I make them laugh?

The pressure on my head lets up. I am brought to sunlight. A warmth on my face, and voices calling to one another but not to me. I have to get my breath. Hurting is not enough to stop me. There is this light. I orient myself to this bright eye-blinding light.

Mr. Baum, we're going to prop you up some more, get some of that fluid broken up in your lungs. We're going to give you a bath now. All right? Can you sit up for me? I'm right here.

A woman's soft arm, not my mother's, pulls me heavily out of my sky.

Mom? I can't see well. Where are you?

1992

After that there is nothing else to say. Like an airport goodbye. We just have to wait.

I would die for a cup of coffee. Live, I mean.

That's it?

Yeah. That's it. I can't have it anymore. With cream. No, a double espresso with a twist. Or a latte. That is what I want. The biggest they have. No. I think just a cup of strong black coffee.

That's all you would come back for? A cup of coffee?

Not just any cup. A bottomless cup.

※

Just for a few moments this one night, I swear I see the nurse's face. I have seen her before. She is a young plump dumpling. Sixteen or sixty-three, I can't tell. She has the brightest blue eyes. She looks right into mine. I see her. I see. I am not supposed to but I do.

Mr. Baum. I would like to give you something to help you sleep. Would you like to sleep?

If I say no, I think I could hurt her feelings. But she is steady and unbroken. There are no wrong answers to her questions.

I think if you could sleep you would get better, she says.

"I am not going to get better," I explain clearly but gently. I keep telling everyone, but they don't believe me. How can she stand there and let my sick breath wash over her when even my friends and lovers stand away? She pats my cold hand with her warm one, and balances a needle in a clear slender barrel between her tiny fingers. I am not supposed to be able to see the short nails on her neat hands, polished a shell pink. The chipped thumbnail. The place on her left cheek where light from the hallway gleams. She raises the needle to eye level and the thumb squeezes the air out until the needle spurts a clear arc. She lowers it to a place I can't see. After I recede from her I know I will never see again. Sometimes I imagine her still standing on a kind of shore, waving waving. My house is surrounded by water.

※

We'll have some high winds as we leave this area, but it should be clear for the remainder of our flight. Just as soon as we're at our desired

1992

altitude we'll turn off the seatbelt sign and you will be free to move about the cabin.

It has been such a long day. A sweet westerly breeze catches me up under the arms and I feel myself lifted by it, an inch or so at first, then several feet off the gravel-topped roof of my building.

What you came for, you will take home. Leave the rest.

※

I can use my arms to steer. Soon I am over my street, passing high over a police van making a bust, the cherry light on top splashing red waves across my chest and legs. I am soaring over the couples, boys and girls and girls and boys, who chatter all along the street, disappearing into clubs, the embers of their cigarettes tracing briskly through the air. I just miss the weather spire on my old office building. I gain altitude over the little park where, carefully, watched by a woman in a sari and a young nanny in shorts, the three remaining children play on the merry-go-round in the early evening air. I just catch the lazy circle the ring-around makes before I pass through a cloud bank, misting my eyes. I turn right and fly above Massachusetts Avenue, over the flags of the embassies, the pinched minarets of the Islamic Center, and finally over the cool treetops along Rock Creek. I exhale until I am low enough to hear the snicker of locusts and the gluey call of a heron. I crash through a few of the tallest tree branches that smell somewhat of car exhaust, but I feel no pain. A familiar dusty smell brushes past my face as I am caressed by the gentle, foul-smelling fronds of the tree of heaven. I am somewhere I haven't been before, flying much lower now. I see familiar things and people I haven't seen for the longest time. I know them all but I can't quite see their faces. I can't name them.

※

We fly but we can't break entirely free. Like kites, we are tethered to our survivors. They hold us in their fists and fly us across their limited horizon. Maybe as time passes, they unroll the cord and let us wind closer to the sun. But we can't be let go until no one on earth remembers the sound of our voices.

1992

The wind in the trees. The light through the leaves. Everywhere. Everywhere. Everywhere.

Did I mention beautiful wrapping paper? Like a warm brown, with a gold ribbon. Always in good taste, but just different enough. Did I mention really good leather? Shoes in particular, I have a closet full, men's size ten and a few women's—who wants them? A clothes hanger full of Mardi Gras beads. Love notes written in haste, in the morning, by the coffee pot or on the refrigerator, once on your car. I kept them. I always wanted to slip one into your hand at a moment's notice.

Schoolyards I occupied: four. College lawns I walked across and lounged on: one. Rooftops I sunned on: an even dozen or more. Places on earth that I lived: three cities, ten dwellings.

Places of worship: perhaps three. Sacraments: three funerals in the immediate family, three weddings, one naming. Or no, if you count childhood, two namings, three circumcisions including my own.

Anniversaries, birthdays, graduations: numerous. Many more memorial services than I care to remark on. You know, I don't want any more fucking flowers.

※

The coloring and shade, the smell and music, some vestige of another moment crowds this one. Then you come back to now, and a moment passes, and another. On and on. Sometimes you know you're making a memory; mostly you don't. In between the best and worst moments, dead space. No. The rests between notes. The knots between pearls. What you came for, what you will take home.

The wind in the trees. The light through the leaves.

This is taking too long.

One more. One more moment. Just one more.

Everything must go.

Gina said once, *I feel sad. We made you a card at school. We took a nature walk. They taught us a new bird.*

You saw a bird?

We heard it. It said hoo-woo, woo, woo.

Do that again.

I have to go.

1992

That's okay. Don't be sad.

I have to go.

Something is missing now. The list in my head. Try to remember what was on it. There were things I wanted to do, and things I had to do, and things I felt I should do. But I can't remember any of them now. I hear the elevator in the hallway open. Would an angel use one? What goes up must come down. The real angels are not invisible, just underfoot. Over us, through us, like light, like air. The ones who bring your newspaper every morning without fail. My angels stand in the doorway, ask the time, make small talk.

Life rushing in. Life rushing out. Hold me. Careful. I can't stand to be touched there.

Breath, of course. And the light in my eyes. Of course that's where it all is. In the light of the eyes. In the breath washing through the heart.

Wake up, sweetie. Wake up.

If you could step outside? We'll handle this. Does he have a DNR?

A what?

Does he want life support?

Oh. Oh. He never would tell us. He wouldn't tell us what he wanted. Okay. That's okay. Just let us take care of him.

※

Am I dead yet? Am I dead? Like a kid in the car. Are we there?

The wind and light travel the earth's circumference. There is no destination but the starting point.

And the eye—of course—the eye is the throne.

※

Professor Van Lare is down below, leading a tour of scribbling youngsters across campus. Dear God, were we ever that young? If I strain I can hear his voice, but there's no need to. I know what he is saying.

The wind in the trees. The light through the leaves.

He is telling them to look up. To keep looking up. I look around instead.

The air is filled with people like the ones in dreams, faces I don't

1992

recognize but seem to know. The harder I look, the more they change, the way the sleeping face of someone you love changes each second and becomes every possible face in the dark.

We aren't in the dark. The sun warms us as we spiral up. We dart and tail each other, always in arcs, the most efficient way to fly. You catch air currents that way.

The group of students on the ground is craning to make out our shapes before we vanish, hands busy across their sketchpads. We are so high up now it would be easier to draw the spaces between us. We wheel above them, out in the open but hidden by the sun that only we can look at directly. The students on the ground must keep looking up in fits and starts, not knowing what they're looking for, not able to see the whole sky. Let them wonder.

We hold our arms open to embrace the light. We don't need to breathe now. It was an inconvenient habit. The air simply moves through us. We don't look up anymore. We don't look down. We are bare limbs held aloft by stars. We are silent. We are where we belong. We are everywhere.

LISA SCHAMESS, a Dallas native and a graduate of Southern Methodist University, has made Washington, D.C., her home since 1987. She is a featured columnist on the Beliefnet Web Site, writing about grief and loss. Her stories have appeared in such venues as *Glimmer Train, Antietam Review,* and *Alabama Fiction Review.* An early draft of *Borrowed Light* earned her the 1995 Jenny McKean Moore Fellowship in Fiction at the Virginia Center for the Creative Arts. As a public policy writer, she has written extensively on urban planning, historic preservation, and transportation. Her work has been published in *Planning, Historic Preservation News,* and *Architectural Record.* She lives with her daughter Mona in a classic Washington rowhouse that needs roof repairs.